ARAM PACHYAN

ROBINSON
SHORT STORIES

PUBLISHED WITH THE SUPPORT
OF THE MINISTRY OF CULTURE OF THE REPUBLIC OF ARMENIA UNDER
THE "ARMENIAN LITERATURE IN TRANSLATION" PROGRAM

ROBINSON: SHORT STORIES

by Aram Pachyan

This book was published with the support
of the Ministry of Culture of the Republic of Armenia under
the "Armenian Literature in Translation" Program

Translated from the Armenian by Nazareth Seferian, Nairi Hakhverdi,
Arevik Ashkharoyan, Nyree Abrahamian, and Lusine Mueller

Edited by Nazareth Seferian

Proofreading by Maria Badanova

Book cover and layout interior created by Max Mendor
Publishers Maxim Hodak & Max Mendor

ISBN: 978-1-912894-75-8

A catalogue record for this book is available from the British Library.

ARAM PACHYAN

ROBINSON
SHORT STORIES

Translated from the Armenian
by Nazareth Seferian, Nairi Hakhverdi, Arevik Ashkharoyan,
Nyree Abrahamian, and Lusine Mueller

GLAGOSLAV PUBLICATIONS

CONTENTS

ROBINSON

I opened the envelope – it was my beloved Friday.

Hello, my master,

I am writing to you from the city of Nantes. After an exhausting journey I have stopped at a comfortable hotel. I had an argument with the staff in the evening because they were stubbornly refusing to take this letter, saying that the era of letters in envelopes was behind us, people only send letters through the internet these days. But, with the stubbornness characteristic of my tribe, I forced them to take the letter and put some money in each of their pockets. I have no good news, master. I stopped at many islands on my journey, one of which seemed so familiar to me that tears started flowing from my eyes, but I later realized that this was simply a case of déjà vu. There was no sign of vegetation left on the island, not even the yellow sand. I was walking on white hot asphalt, burning my feet. There were factories all around me making terrifying noises, there were no parrots or goats – I came across no animals in any case, not even a mosquito. I was thirsty and looked for gushing springs, but it was all in vain. Master, I was in for a surprise. I stood in front of a café that was called Robinson. I sat down and ordered some water, but they refused to serve me. They said, "We are running out of water on the island and if you're not a factory employee, you have no right to ask for drinking water. Besides, everyone must smile on this island – this is a mandatory requirement. If you don't obey this law, you will be subjected to terrible punishment." "What do you mean?" I was surprised. "I mean that, if you don't smile, the corners of your mouth will be sewn with surgical thread to the lobes of your ears." A stupid smile appeared immediately on my face, master. The fear I felt caused me pain. I sat for a while in the café and realized that the bartender was being nice to me. When there were fewer customers left, he brought me a waterlike liquid.

I put money in his pocket and expressed my gratitude. I left that island with a heavy heart and then landed in many other islands that did not differ from each other – there were people everywhere that were waging a war against sorrow, but the most terrifying thing was the noise to which they were now accustomed, and they slept soundly even though it went all the way up to space. There is nowhere in the world where I can make a ship and come for you; I know that you have been waiting impatiently for years in the belief that I will tap on your window one day. I have not lost hope yet. I'm going to leave for Canada from here where I will look for a tree to make a barka. But master, even if I manage to make one, have you thought about the direction in which we need to point our compass, what we need to do, where we need to search for the island? These are worrying questions; I pray every day for you to find peace. Master, I hope the time when we meet is near, please keep the necessary trunks ready.

With love,
Yours, Friday.

I dipped my pen into the inkwell and wrote a letter in response.

Dearest Friday,

I felt unbounded joy when I saw your slanted handwriting – emotional, worrying about me. I am also searching for the island in my room full of books in Yerevan, under the plaster, between the covers, in my hair. I drink a washing soda solution at dawn, throw up, use the tip of my pen to poke at porridge and the fresh excreta of my family members, but the island is not there, as if it never existed. How ungrateful I had been when I was complaining of my solitude and cursing that magnificent island, where my good fortune had given me refuge...[1] *In my dreams I come close to that familiar shore, but when I step into that sand, I leap out of bed with fever, I see Jesus and wildly tear his belly, pulling out his intestines, but I cannot find the island. Then, drained by my powerlessness, I cut my skin with a knife and my nerves flutter like sails in the wind. But where*

----

[1]   Daniel Defoe, *Robinson Crusoe* (Oxford; New York: Oxford University Press, 2007).

is the island? The island is not here either. I look in the mirror and think that perhaps this is the island, without trees or shores, without the sea or wind.

Dear Friday, I am suffering from a strange disease. My hands are growing shorter and it is becoming difficult for me to write these lines. Perhaps this is endocrine in nature, or a case of visual schizophrenia. I'm shrinking.

When I returned home, everyone was happy. Two days later, they gave me a mobile phone, a black suit, and sent me to work in an office. The phone kept ringing without interruptions. It got to me and I switched it off, then threw it under a fireproof drawer so that I would not hear its noise, but I got a scolding at home for doing this.

"The whole world is looking for you, irresponsible creature," my father shouted, "You have no right to switch off your mobile phone."

"I'm in no condition to answer all these calls," I protested to my father.

"Nobody cares about the condition you're in," he stormed, "People are looking for you."

"I'm not used to all this yet. I need time. I want to be alone sometimes because I miss the island."

"What island? Your boss came over last evening and said that you hadn't shown up for work. Where were you? The city is looking for you, do you understand, you idiot?"

Father slapped me.

"If you switch off your phone again, I'll kill you!"

Blood flowed from my lip.

"Where is the island?" I asked.

He put a finger on his temple and screamed.

"It's in here, in here!"

I walked up to him and examined his head carefully. My father's fist landed on my jaw and I felt a pleasant pain. "Perhaps this blow will dispatch me to the island," I thought.

Dearest Friday, Jesus and I stand near the window every day, waiting for the ripples caused by your boat... And by the way, it makes no difference whether it is a large boat or a small one...[2]

I embrace you warmly. Hurry!"[3]

....

[2]   Hovhannes Grigoryan, *Robinson Crusoe*.

[3]   Julio Cortázar, *Adiós, Robinson* (Alfaguara, 2018).

* * *

The room where I've relocated is similar to a Bible with a worn leather cover, which smells of moisture. This is where I hide my books, there is almost no place to walk except for three intersecting paths, one of which leads to the bed, the other to the window, and the third to the wall, against which leans a crate of bananas. I don't leave my room for months, trying not to cause any inconvenience to my family members living in the apartment. My books have grown in number so much that there is no longer any place for my feet, I somehow managed to curl up on the windowsill, trying to avoid unnecessary movement; I don't cough, sneeze or go to the bathroom, I try not to breathe because the pile of books that are stacked up to the ceiling hangs above my head like the sword of Damocles, a small tremor and it will be difficult to pull my body out from that heavy mass. I have quite a large stock of ink and the goosefeather pen is so light that it feels like one of my own fingers. I eat a banana every day and collect the skins, which I use as the pages of my diary. Bananas do not understand Shakespearean language… but they fill my humble belly. I am full of wonder – how is it that the crate of bananas never empties? I meticulously fill out my diary in the silence afforded by the books.

* * *

March 19. Friday. The boys were using cigarettes to burn the teacher's nose – this was the last action in the ceremony. They had crucified the teacher on the blackboard. One of them had covered the teacher's mouth with his palm. The old educator was screaming, her voice filtering through the boy's fingers and sounding like the whistle of a boiling kettle. The girls were applying make-up to their faces and whispering to each other, their cosmetics strewn on the table. I could not leave the classroom, the door was locked tight. The old teacher was floundering with the jerky movements of a sheep being slaughtered, trying to escape the tongs. The hot breath of the cigarette moved slowly like lava across her nose. Tears were streaming from her eyes. The boys called out to me and asked me to come closer and grab her left leg, which was impudently refusing to behave itself. I did not move from my spot. The cigarette singed the random hairs growing on her nose and touched her skin, filling the room with the smell of cooking meat and the teacher's indescribable scream. "Only newborns scream like that," I thought. The pain gave the old teacher the immense strength she needed to break free from the boys' grasp, and she chose the window with lightning speed and threw herself out. We saw her lying there, on the sole rock in all that grass, shattered. But, her belief in resurrection allowed her to get up and run away, disappearing in the stream of people on the crowded street. Someone opened the classroom door, I wanted to walk out but a book dropped out from under my coat at that moment…

"Oh dear…"

"No, no, take a good look at this colorful picture – Robinson, with a gun on his shoulder, his mangy mutt in the river, and a stupid parrot perched on his head. This guy is about to start the tenth grade and here he is, hiding a book about Robinson under his coat, concealing it from us. That's why you weren't helping us, isn't it?" the boy continued, his long face scowling, "Grab him!"

The classroom door closed from the inside. One of the boys picked the book up from the floor, brought it to his mouth and began to lick the cover. They surrounded me. The execution began. The blows landed with the rough impact of a blunt ax on a tree trunk, scratching away at the bark. Whitish blood surged from my eyes, nose, and ears. "It must be because of the bananas," I thought. From where I lay on the ground, I cast half a glance and noticed how the girls were popping the pimples on their faces in front of egg-shaped mirrors. One of the boys was extremely offended and found himself unable to calm down. He picked up some chalk and stuffed my mouth with it, forcing me to chew it and swallow. Then he picked up a bench and turned it over on my head. I lay there on the parqueted floor. I felt a craving for fruits and soft wool. Some time later, they grabbed me by the armpits and dragged me to the bathroom. The stink of urine and shit from the ceramic tiles forced me to refocus. A pale boy brought the book closer to my eyes and stabbed the cover with a knife he had in his pocket. Then each of them walked up one by one and ripped pages from the book, stuffing them into the toilet bowl. When the last page floated down like a feather to the top of that pyramid, one of the boys lowered his pants and showered the pages with an abundant stream of urine, scattering them around.

* * *

March 19. Friday. The wind blows shadows and raises waves, striking against the rocky cliff… Why don't the ghosts of boats leave you in peace? The children curled up in them float to your window, the faces they make imprinting themselves on your foggy window. The wind paints illusions with dust which emit pathological giggles, rubbing their faces against yours. They all invite you to their boats, freeing up some space inside. You cover your face with your sandy palms. You're scared. They tap on the wet window and invite you to the ballroom of the wind, and out there, later, the island awaits you as a father waits for his son. Rocking in a swing, you anchor in the bay and throw yourself in the water, so that you can feel the warmth of that familiar shore a few meters away. You then rush to your hut, close the door tightly, blocking it with large stones. You jump at a strange sound in the night. The children have surrounded your hut, they are knocking on your door with their dolls, calling out to you. They have come to your island, they're afraid of being alone, scared of the ugly silhouettes of mountains and rocks. Panic takes root in their souls. They are knocking on the door. The dolls' faces have been mangled by the blows, strands of their hair caught in the cracks between the pieces of wood. Dark water flows from beneath the door like a tired black snake, bringing with it the childrens' faces… You will not be alone on your island any more… You will no longer fish alone, you will not die alone, you will not talk to God alone, hear the songs of the fish and snails, walk beneath the clear sky, be a shadow, lying down to get some rest. There is nothing left here except these ominous sounds that are filling your mouth so abundantly, your ears, nose, navel, the space between your fingernails, under your skin, inside your eyelids. This island, living in sound, drives you insane, each animal and plant has taken on a human shape, even the countless grains of sand, the nearly invisible grains of sand, have faces like witches, all of them sighing with relief as they come across your footprint. If you leave now, you will be surrounded by millions of swinging boats, you will hear the cries of children, see the cracked heads of their dolls, the dark traces of their blood… "Stay in your rickety hut, don't give in to that fake sobbing, do not open your door under any circumstances, don't feel sorry for the children, they're tricksters!"… "Open the door, they're your friends, your parents, your family, the ones you love…" You miss the cannibals from before, the human sharpness of their knives, their insatiable appetites, the acrid smell of their spices, which they had used to cover your body… They are no longer here either. This is not your island…

The waves crash against the walls of the room – the apartment will collapse any moment now. The boat is loaded with barrels of fresh water, food rations, and then it distances itself in the cold waves and vanishes into non-existence.

"You're an idiot. You keep looking out the window all day, I'm going to take you to a psychiatrist… Look at me!"

I looked.

"Your face… Beaten up again…"

"The girls from your class called and said that the boys had beaten you up again."

"Nothing happened, I'm trying to sleep…"

"I want us to have a talk…"

"We'll talk tomorrow, I'm already in bed…"

"Who was that tapping on your bedroom window?"

"The wind…"

"There's no wind at this time, you idiot…"

"There is."

"You fool…"

I took out a ripe banana from the box, peeled it, and gave the delicious pulp to Jesus. I needed to stay hungry, so that I could revive my memories. I dipped my pen into the inkwell.

* * *

March 19. Friday. The children hated the little boy because he had a limp and his mother was a whore. The women in the yard would say, "Only whores dye their hair blonde," "Only whores take a bath every day," "Only whores get a divorce." They did not like the Woman because she did not smell of sweat, she was always pretty and clean. As she walked, her wheat-colored skin left aromatic clouds of delicious soaps and fragrant perfumes. As opposed to the other women in the Vegetable Market District, she did not have a mustache and did not burn her armpit hair on a gas fire – she went to the hairdresser. That woman had mastered the art of putting her body on display. She wore neat dresses in mild colors, emphasizing her magnificent breasts, back, waist… Her toes were delicate as pomegranate seeds, and clean. She also had kind eyes. After divorcing her authoritarian husband at a young age, she had inherited a son and a ramshackle two-story house. She had never attempted marriage again, earning the reputation of an immoral woman. She would leave the house in the morning to run errands and return home late at night, a bag of fruits or vegetables in hand. Sometimes, the little boy and his mother would bump into each other in the stairwell, when the child was taking his guinea pig downstairs to the yard to munch some grass. The boy was sickly. His body was misshapen, he had a large head with hair that stuck out, his eyes were a sensitive green and always looked downwards. He had tried a long time ago to make friends with the other children, when he had stepped into the yard to play football with them…

He walked slowly up to the playground, looking nervously at the children that were rolling about on top of each other.

When the dust settled and the ball rolled up to the boy's feet, everyone fell silent.

"Look, the ghost has arrived."

"…"

"Hi, bogeyman!"

The boy was staring at a bottlecap stuck in the mud.

"You're the son of a whore… Your mother's a whore," one boy said, his finger up his nose.

"You dream of playing with us all day, don't you?" the fat kid continued, "But you're retarded and lame, right?"

"…"

"…"

"Yes," the boy's sad voice came out. In his mind, he was counting the scratches on the bottlecap's surface. Then he turned around and slowly walked away.

"Lame-o, lame-o, lame-o," the children shouted after him, throwing small stones at his back, his head, and shoulders. The boy stopped, bent over, collected all the stones, poured them into his pocket and continued to walk away. He did not come down to the yard after that. People said that the boy's illness grew more and more severe after that. But I knew better – the children's indifference had been the real reason why his face had grown crooked, why his hair had grown thinner. He was like a plant on the windowsill, looking sadly at the shadows playing in the street. His quiet isolation angered the other children. They threw stones at the window of his room, and drowned his mother with questions about the boy: "Does he or does he not have a bicycle?", "Does he or does he not have a father?", "When is he going to die?", "Why doesn't he leave the house?", "Why doesn't he talk?", "Whose plant is that on the windowsill?", "Is that a boy or girl?" Instead of replying, his mother would use her fingers to bring her fluffs of hair to her ears and quicken her pace. "I don't have time for this, no time at all, kids," she would say and click her heels as she walked to the bus stop.

The children would be unable to calm down. One would propose going to the boy's room late at night, strangling him and then hanging him out on the clotheslines for his mother to see, another would suggest tearing his belly open, putting the guinea pig in there and sewing it back up, or checking to see whether he had a tongue, then cutting it, barbecuing it and feeding it to him, or trying to saw off his hands and legs, then putting him on the ground face down so that he would suffocate from the loss of blood. I did not like any of the recommended options. I felt sorry for the little boy. In my mind, I kept thinking about painless ways to kill him, like giving him the most delicious poison in the world, pretending to accidentally run him over with my bicycle, playing so much with him that his heart bursts with joy, growing his legs so that he can run, and then watching him run so much that he reaches the sky.

When Jesus blinked, it scared me. He was looking out the window. I was intrigued by the way he stared. I looked out as well. In the yard of the two-story house, the lame boy was sitting in the green grass, his guinea pig grazing in the space between his legs. The electric lamp flickered with his movements. I put the pen and ink in my pocket and stepped outside, Jesus came with me. We approached them shyly. The boy did not move, he was looking at the guinea pig that was eating juicy timothy grass.

"Hello…"

"…"

"I saw that you were outside the house and I came downstairs to see you…"

"…"

"You have to be careful of the other kids, they want to kill you…"

"…"

"Can't you speak, or do you simply not want to?"

"…"

"I was thinking that, if you don't want to speak, you can write on this banana skin. I'll write too. I'll give you a pen and some ink…"

"…"

He was rubbing the animal's soft belly.

"Fine, if you agree, then I'll give the answers to my questions in your place…"

"…"

Jesus perched on the boy's shoulders. "He's light." "Yes, he's very old. I bought him from the market last year." "Why him in particular?" "I don't know. I dreamed of having a friend. When I saw Jesus, I took a liking to him immediately." "Does he speak?" "No, he doesn't speak at all, he can't fly either. If he wants to escape now, he won't be able to, his wings are very weak, he's already eighteen years old." "Just like me… I don't talk and can't fly either, I would have escaped this place immediately if I had been able to fly." "Where would you go?" "I would escape to the place from which Jesus has come." "Jesus hasn't come from anywhere, he was caught by some hunters off the coast of Madagascar and brought to the Vienna zoo. After several years of extreme effort, the trainers understood that he will never be able to speak and they sold him to a Diaspora Armenian who brought him to Armenia and gifted him to a rich family. When they saw that Jesus was disabled, they took him to the market, which is where I bought him for a hundred dollars." "Jesus is very good." "The children want to kill you." "Never mind." "They want to hang you from the clothesline so that your mother sees you in the morning." "Would that satisfy them?" "I don't know, but don't you want to protect yourself?" "I don't know how to protect myself." "Lash out with your arms and legs, bite them." "I don't know how to hit people. Why do they want to kill me?" "Because you manage to live alone, without any games." "I wanted to make friends with them, but they didn't want to." "They wanted you to cry, to beg them, beseech them for friendship, but you ended up quietly leaving." "But I'm alone in my room now, I never leave. Why would they want to kill me?" "They can't feel completely happy while you're alone in your room, because they keep remembering you and want to kill you, so that nobody stays alone in the world." "But why don't they want to kill you or Jesus?" "They've already killed us, but the fools don't realize it." "I would love to live with my guinea pig on an uninhabited island, like Robinson." "Don't waste your time on that dream, there aren't any uninhabited islands anymore. You will be found and killed wherever you go." "If only I could die like you and Jesus, so that they wouldn't be able to kill me." "For that to happen, you would have to be sad all the time – constantly, constantly, sad forever." "I'm always sad." "In that case, you'll die soon. The most painless way to die in the world is sorrow." "When I die, will I be forgotten?" "You'd have to be really sad for a long time after your death as well if you don't want to ever be remembered. They say that many children look out your window, umbrellas in hand." "I'm the only one in my room." "You have a pretty beard." "You too." "Retarded children end up with thick facial hair that develops early." "But you aren't retarded." "I *am* retarded. That's what everyone says." "That's fine, Robinsons are always retarded. Look, Jesus likes you, he's not stepping down from your shoulders." "Jesus is very nice. It's too bad we got to know each other so late, I'll miss him. Have you come to see me off?" "I want to make sure you don't feel scared and alone. You're not scared, are you?" "No." "Shall we go?" "Let's go."

* * *

The sound of shattering glass awoke the sleeping inhabitants. People ran out to their balconies, looking carefully at the section of pavement where the crystals were shining like little stars. "What happened? What happened to my son?" "Open the door, open it," "Help, anyone!" the lady from apartment 24 was shouting. "Open the door," "Break it open, break the door…" A police car and ambulance took turns overtaking each other as they rushed into the yard. The rescue workers ran into the apartment, where they were met by a beautiful woman with a face the color of clay, who pointed to a room – "My son is in there, in there!" The door was firmly shut. They used a hammer and metal chisel to break the lock. The room shuddered and was lost in a cloud of dust. When the dust settled, nobody managed to get past the entrance. Everyone was surprised – was it really possible to arrange so many books in such a small space? "He's under those books, he's beneath them! Pull him out, pull him!" the woman howled. Everyone started to empty the room in a rush. The rescue team was lost in a cloud, they had been working for half an hour, but there was no end in sight to the books. Soon, the wet floorboards could be seen. "There's nobody here." They walked up to the window. The glass was completely shattered, a wonderful cool breeze was blowing in from the gap. The windowpane was wet.

The police detective was at work outside. He was carefully examining the small pieces of broken glass, then placing them in a plastic bag for further tests. It was the first time that he had seen such a case – it looked like suicide, but there was no body. They searched the whole building, the dogs grew exhausted, but they could not find a single trace of blood. The ambulance soon departed, taking the crazed woman, who had started to recite poetry. The young detective lit a cigarette with a trembling hand, gathered his things and, raising his head, looked up at the window on the ninth floor. "If someone jumps out of the window now, I'll quickly move aside," he thought to himself and went up to his office. There were squished banana skins on various parts of the floor. A bright red spot appeared on the windowsill. The detective narrowed his eyes and walked up to it. The red spot was moving. It was a small fish the size of a strawberry, floundering in agony. He took a sample from the water and banana skin, found a cake box full of small stones, and packed them all. His phone rang.

"There's no body…"

"What do you mean, there isn't? What are you saying, you idiot?"

"We've looked everyone, even in the yards of neighboring buildings."

"A kidnapping?"

"I don't think so. His mother was home and said that she had spoken to her son ten minutes before the incident…"

"What do the neighbors say?"

"All they heard was the sound of breaking glass and a dull thud…"

"Then the mother must have killed the child, that must be it. She must have hidden him somewhere. Have you searched the apartment well? Checked the fridge? Maybe she stuffed him there…"

"We've searched everywhere in the apartment, he's not there…"

"Listen, I don't care, you have to find the body before dawn…"

"How can I find it if it's not there?"

"Find it, you fool! Die if you must but find it first. Understood? If you don't find it, you'll end up in prison tomorrow…"

He stopped breathing and stared indifferently at the trash can in front of him. He sighed, ended the call, picked up his bags and left.

He bought a mushroom salad and dry wine from a shop on the way, thinking that the food and drink would dull his senses. The car stopped beneath the gray wall of the summer house. He somehow managed to drag himself out of the car and opened the door. He stood in the middle of the blue living room for a few moments like a marble statue, then sat down on the couch, turned on some music and opened the bottle. Davis' trumpet and the wine mixed into his blood like a drug, flowing through his veins, numbing all his senses. Images spun around his head like lampposts. He saw flying children whose milky necks were strangled by tight threads. They were smiling… "Why do children die? What do they feel when they are flying?" "Poor children…"

He stepped out, walked into the depths of the park, sat in the black grass, and started talking to himself. The mosquitoes lusciously bit his legs. He was slipping into a profound numbness, but he was afraid to greet the dawn. What would he say? They knocked on his door. His body had grown heavy. They knocked again. Who could that be? The detective did not move from his spot. He poured a handful of soil into his hair and mouth. Had they really found him? "They don't know where this summer house is," "Nobody knows." The knocking on the door grew louder. His skin began to flutter. He turned back and went into the bedroom, trying to dance the Irish twist, "Nobody knows where the summer house is," "Nobody." When his feet grew tired, he leaned on a wall. He heard the knocking at the door. He ran to the living room, turned up the volume of the music and buried himself in the couch. "But, nobody knows." When the music ended, he heard the knocking again. From where he sat, his feet stretched like plane trees, reaching all the way up to the front door. He moved forward slowly, standing fearfully in front of the door and pulled back the bolt with bated breath… A boy stood in the dark, holding a guinea pig, eating a large apple with noisy bites. The detective had frozen in place, tried to speak, to say a word, but only ended up listening.

"Your boat has arrived…"

"What boat?"

"Your boat…"

"Who are you, boy?" he giggled, his legs were trembling.

"…"

"…"

"…"

"It's time, let's go…"

The little boy grabbed his moist pinky finger. They walked.

JOURNEY BY BICYCLE

She stroked my cheek with her fingers, put the sweet, tasty cotton candy in my hand, smiled, and talked a little with my mother... The sweet cotton candy did not reduce the magic of that moment... Big black nipples winked from her transparent white bra... My body replied... Unfortunately, it was still too early for an erection... I felt the remainder with the palm of my hand, rubbed it thoroughly when I got home, and washed myself with soap, but nothing came out... I plucked my skin with a towel... Bloody blisters... Mom got worried:

"Who hit you?"

"No one... It scraped against a branch while I was eating mulberries, mom..."

Auntie Lia was there during the earthquake, the rallies, the bread with ration coupons, the warm hot water bottles, the heater, the watching of soap operas using battery power, the tearless funerals, and she became, unnoticeably and innocently, the most desirable guest of my dreams... I was not at all interested in the lives of the residents of our courtyard, but willingly and unwillingly I was apprised of the latest and freshest news: the tattling mothers were the guilty ones – it was simply unbearable when they got together for coffee, impossible to concentrate on my homework...

"My mother-in-law is driving me crazy! She's started soiling herself. Why doesn't she just die?"

"So have you heard? Lia's husband has been appointed a judge..."

"Girls, I'm going to the gynecologist tomorrow. I want to get an IUD..."

I had studiously memorized everyone's intimate relationships – my age allowed me to listen in to such stories like a class auditor... Any broken toy was an excuse for me... Lia's name whetted my senses... When I was playing in one corner or another of the courtyard, I would freeze for a moment and let her scent soak into me like warm asphalt soaking up rainwater... My rickety bicycle had changed its course. As soon as it came out of 21st Street, the asphalt was replaced by Lia's milky-white skin... It would roll over Lia's body, roll up and down her delicate creases, the bicycle, leading itself, had forgotten all about me, its loyal owner...

We lived like relatives, all of us sharing whatever we had and didn't have, but Lia's family set themselves apart... The position of her husband the judge required other values and other people that weren't like us... The first rumbles of a petrol generator in the building were heard from apartment 19. Auntie Lia's son, Arman, would go to school wearing jeans. Even their garbage was different – I had examined it secretly... My ideas of Auntie Lia's family and their lifestyle were elaborate... In my mind I would go to their apartment, participate in their merry parties, savor the fried chicken with mushrooms, sprawl in their leather armchair... I was sure that in their house you would never hear things like "there's nothing to eat," "we've run out of candles," "we're sorry for your loss," "I wish your father were here"... New, pleasant changes had also started in me... When I lay in bed and thought about her, the thing between my legs, which had started to embarrass me, would fill with warmth... My new world had nothing to do with chopping firewood, with the arguments at home, and with me in general... All of this was like listening to a movie on the radio when, reinforcing the scene in your head, you start to see the images... I wasn't alone then; my happiness comprised three letters, where no permit allowed entry... At night I slept in the little leather bag attached to the back of my bicycle. It was comfortable there; besides, no one at home could see what kept their son busy – that made me incredibly happy... Questions had arisen in me involving naked bodies and strange visions, but these were answers that aroused doubt and did not satisfy my insatiable curiosity... I asked my mother with an innocent look on my face about the details of coming into the world: "a stork brought you," "Santa Claus brought you as a gift," "we plucked you out of a cabbage"... I would nod, as if I really believed it, but when I tried to get more specific, they would scold me and send me to buy bread, and I would get annoyed, lose my courage, and have no other choice but to pick up the facts from street education – rough and wild... I remember my classmate, a pretty girl called Esther, who had a weakness for candy... I would take her to a quiet place after class... Candy... She would pull up her skirt... Candy... She would pull down her underwear... Her pink crack, with all its magic, would smile heartily... I was convinced that the beginning and the end was a pink crack, the source of life, the road to heaven... I had become absorbed, lost in my own secret game, forgetting everyone, noticing nothing around me – the bathroom had become my latest stop, from which it was beyond my powers to unchain myself... But one day I got my fingers burned: my father caught me... He caught me and beat me, in an unrefined sort of way... The beating was horrible; I couldn't walk for days... A pity... My father did not live long. Maybe he would have understood that beating me at the time only widened the abyss separating us in our relationship, but he probably wouldn't have... Even later, he and I never grew close... The word "close" did not exist in our dictionaries at all; we were only alike in terms of resemblance and last names... He would always say that I was an apple that had rolled far from the tree and then laugh at me... He would never listen to me and that was the main reason for my estrangement... But I love him...

One day I heard an exchange that rocked my world... There was a chubby boy who lived in our courtyard, a child of prospering parents... When he talked, he always deliberately belched and what was interesting was that his father always encouraged that behavior and said, "What do you want me to buy for you, dear child?" and we would hear, "Hm... grrr... Sni... burp... ckers... Snickers... burp..." and so on... But he had a more serious fault: he was a born thief. Even though he had the latest, most expensive bicycle models, he would steal our old and rickety bike, assembled from the various parts of different bicycles... Once again, my bicycle had disappeared, and even the toddlers crawling about the courtyard knew who the thief was... It was interesting – every week, he would steal a few bicycles, take them to the entrance of his building, line them up in a row and, greedily devouring a Snickers, rivet his dreamy eyes on their twisted corpses, their misshapen wheels of various sizes, but what was most unbearable was taking back the bicycle from that riveted stare; a sharp, ear-piercing shriek would shake the whole building... The boy would fall to the ground, bawl and cry, and then his father would beat him long and hard, and, foaming at the mouth, say: "You beastly child, don't you have enough bikes? Why are you collecting these broken bikes and bringing them here, eh?"

The boy bribed me a few times with peach yoghurt; one ride around the courtyard in exchange for one yoghurt, but in the end he got annoying, taking my bicycle wherever he wanted... Now go try to find it... It had disappeared yet again, and I knew whose hands had done it... I went up to the last floor to get my bicycle... I was coming down the stairs when Auntie Lia's voice reached me through a crack in her apartment door...

"Enough already, tell those whores of yours not to call here anymore... You have no shame... Arman already understands everything! At least be ashamed in front of him!"

"Scream... Louder! You want the neighbors to hear this, don't you?"

"Yeah, let them hear it, let them hear it and understand that the most miserable woman in this building is me..."

"Miserable? Man, if anyone asked, where does anyone live the kind of life you have? For God's sake..."

"I hate this life... I couldn't care less about the money you bring – someone else's blood and sweat..."

"Shut your mouth!"

The slap did not stop Lia's voice...

"Kill me if you want, it's all the same to me now, I'm sick of this disgraceful life... Every other day I get a call, 'Lia, your husband is cheating on you,' 'Lia, what is this we hear? They say your husband is taking whores to Marriott Hotel...' That's not you? At least have the decency to cover it up so that no one finds out..."

"But I do it precisely so that they know and you know... No, I know your pain, you want to get laid, you haven't done it in a long time... That's what you want, period..."

"Oh my goodness! Oh my goodness!"

I ran out into the courtyard with sweat dripping down my forehead... Lia, bicycle, cotton candy, Esther, leather bag... They all faced off against the words "you want to get laid"... I thought for days after that, I wanted to understand, to analyze, to sort the reasons in my head, but nothing came out of it, and there was nothing left to do but be sad... Being sad is always an option and now, even more so, the urge was stronger; after all, Lia was sad, and sadness was like the cookies given out in school – you bite it enthusiastically and end up leaving a tooth in it... I wanted to walk up to her and say, "don't be sad by yourself, it'll be easier together," but I didn't dare and had no other choice but to pass it on telepathically...

I graduated from school one way or another and I had to gain admission to university, so I took private lessons... Life had changed after the ceasefire... The changes were new and interesting, but also tedious... Lia hardly ever appeared; she was leading the life of a hermit, she did not come down to the courtyard, did not mingle with our mothers, sometimes it seemed to me as if she had never existed, as if she had only been a figment of my imagination; her husband had grown a huge belly, as if he were a pregnant woman... He would trudge out of his office car, staring ahead of him, looking for the wizened old women who greeted him several times a day just to make their helloes reach a destination... With full plastic bags from Orchard Supermarket in his hands, he would go into the entrance slowly and walk up to the apartment, counting the stairs... How much I wanted for us to exchange places just once! I would ring the doorbell, and a few seconds later, Lia would open the door, but I don't know why, right there, her face would shatter and I never managed to pick up the last little shard that would complete the picture...

We took English language classes in a group – four boys and three girls, one of whom I was not indifferent to... She always wore brightly colored clothes, short skirts... Once in a while we laughed as soon as she appeared in the distance, we would say, "the prissy princess is here, hold your breath..." She always used Russian words when she talked, probably to appear modern... In class, she callously drove me crazy, scratching her breasts in front of me, slowly pulling up her skirt, winking, in a word, trying to tell me something... I started to collect money, I took loans from my friends, sold my bike's Bosch bell to Pushko, and imagined that I had gathered quite a bit of capital... After class, I followed her and didn't let her cross the street...

"Hey, Sona, wait a sec, there's something I want to tell you..."

She calmly stopped; she had probably been waiting for this for a while...

"*Nu, skazhi* – so tell me, what is it?"

She brushed her hair back from her brow...

"I'd like to take you out somewhere. Will you come?"

"*Ty*, you, are asking me out somewhere? Good boy, and where would that be?"

"Well, you decide, I don't know..."

"*Tak, tak, tak*, okay, okay, *nu ladno*, well, *esli tak*, in that case, *poydyom v karaoke*, let's go do karaoke, I want to sing a little... but don't bring that *razvalina*, wrecked bicycle of yours, it's embarrassing..."

                                                ARAM PACHYAN

I listened; I left my bicycle with my friends and we walked to Prospekt... I was tense, I felt empty inside... No sooner did we walk in than the waiter appeared before us with a tray...

"What would you like?"

"A 'Masquerade' cocktail, a Bologna pizza, some freshly-squeezed orange juice, popcorn, a fruit plate, and... the list of songs..."

I could not help coughing...

"And for *you*?"

"I'll have a black coffee, man..."

More and more food kept coming to our table, Sona was having fun, stroking my hair with her thin fingers...

"*Kak ti, malchik moy*, how are you, my boy? I want a cocktail..."

She grew tipsy... She sang all of Alla Pugachova's songs, but towards the end it was just a bunch of random shouting, she had drunk a lot... I quietly asked for the bill, and when the waiter brought it, the pupils of my eyes dilated: 25,100 drams... I broke out in a cold sweat, I drank a gulp of juice, what was I going to do? I held my stomach...

"Sona, Sona..."

"*Da, malchik moy*, yes, my boy..."

"Sona, my stomach hurts... I'm going to the bathroom for a minute..."

"*Nu, davai*, okay, go..."

I ran out... I hailed a *marshrutka* and went to Komitas Avenue... Ten minutes later I was in our neighborhood... Khryush was squatting under a wall...

"Hey, man, what's up? I need some money until tomorrow, help me, will you?" I said.

"Ar *jan*, I've taken all my jewelry to the pawnshop, these are bad times for me, man, sorry. Go to the car wash, maybe the guys will have some..."

I was embarrassed: how could I ask those boys for money when they worked all day like slaves? No, I couldn't ask them... What should I do, what should I do? The thought that was born in my head scared me, but the fear felt very pleasant, for the first time I wished to properly feel fear, it was like being run over by a car, when you somehow avoid the blow and manage to calm down afterwards... How I went, I don't know... Did I go, did my childhood go? I don't know. I knocked on the apartment door of number 19 and Lia opened it...

"Hello, Aram *jan*..."

"..."

"Aram *jan*, what happened? You look pale..."

"Auntie Lia, can you lend me some money?"

"Of course I'll give you some. Come in. How much do you need, Aram *jan*?"

"...Thirty-thou-ousand drams. I'll b-ring it b-ack in a few d-days..."

"Bring it back whenever you can, okay?"

She smiled... She soon brought the money and put in my hand. I didn't have time to relax, I found myself at the bus stop again, half an hour had already gone by, it was becoming quite long for a bathroom visit, so I got a taxi to the karaoke bar... I went in, Sona was fighting with the manager, she saw me and cackled...

"*Malchik moy*, my boy, were you laying eggs in that bathroom? I want a Malibu..."

"It's time for us to leave, Son *jan*..."

I paid the bill and dragged her out by the arms barely able to convince her. She had taken the microphone with her and was starting to give a concert in the middle of the street. I somehow managed to get it out of her hands and return it to the terrified waiter running after us... On the way back, she started to curse the taxi driver for driving slowly. I got her home somehow... My first date came to an end, my bicycle had ended up without a bell... I took Lia's money from the sum meant for my tutor's payment. At home, I said I had lost it on the bus and they believed me... I put on my school graduation suit, sprayed some Cigar cologne, brushed my hair with green gel, looked in the mirror for a long time, took the money, and went to Lia's house... When she opened the door, I was shaking...

"Hi, Aram *jan*, come in..."

Trying to keep my cool, I walked in, walked up to the leather armchair, and sat down... As I passed the window, my gaze fell on the roof of the opposite building, from which I had watched the closed windows of apartment 19 for hours on end... There was no fried chicken with mushrooms on the table... Lia was wearing black pajamas, home alone... She got whiskey from the bar, poured it into triangular tumblers, walked up to me, gave me one, and sat down next to me... She was very sad...

"Aram *jan*, why are you sad?"

We drank whiskey...

"Arman went to England to study, and left me here alone..."

"You are not alone..."

She embraced my neck, and I don't want to remember what happened next... I loved her, I loved myself... At that moment I wasn't even thinking that the Armenian warrior of justice could come in at any moment... If only the knot didn't break... I told her my sweet wet dreams and secret deeds, where she was the center of the plot... and I loved, loved, loved with all the strength that I had... She told me that for ten years there had not been a man in her life, she apologized and cried for a long time... After that we met a few times, all we did was talk, we recalled the old neighbors of our courtyard, we looked at some photographs... I promised her I would forget everything, but I lied... I passed my exams successfully and got into university... When I received her last message, it was snowing, the flake resembled Lia's face... She had divorced the judge and had moved to Malta...

"I will feel and you will sit in an outdoor café, drink coconut juice with a straw, and for a moment you will think about Komitas Avenue and me... I will feel this as I'm writing down what the lecturer dictates and, holding my pen tightly, I'll scratch the paper..."

When my bicycle was dying, I held its handles, it was impossible to bring it back to life, so I decided to let it turn to dust. I took it to the river gorge and, from a convenient hilltop, let it roll down, and then I sat on the ground and smoked... My next journey started by car...

CHESS NOVEL

> To my eternal brother, Karen Asryan
> Hello Karen, is everything ok? (SMS)

"It was like the question of what exists and what does not, as everything is, nobody knows that he exists, but he does. Like with God, for example. Nobody knows that he exists, but he is talking now, you can be sure of it. Do you have a smoke? I like strong cigarettes."

I offered the old man a slim; he complained, but he had not choice, he took it and lit it immediately.

"You know, I don't like noise, I'm an irritable person, I need silence to calculate my next move. Real sound comes from within silence, from emptiness, blackness, from zero, it comes carefully, lighting matches along the way. You have to be careful to capture it, grab it tightly, like a fly resting on your elbow, don't doubt that if you manage to do this, you will never be fooled by it. You will hear the sound again – the one that existed before but you could not hear – and you will only make your famous move after it comes."

The old man fell silent. His thick-framed glasses with large lenses hung from his sun-peeled sharp nose. Saryan Park was busy, the benches were all occupied by people. He took out his dirty, wrinkled handkerchief from the pocket of his brown pants, rubbed it with his hand a few times to soften it, and then brought it to his nose with all the enthusiasm and fastidiousness he could muster. He squeezed out all of its inner contents, emptied it out, folded the handkerchief several times, and put it back in his pocket.

"They say that the boy beat his father at the age of four, while his father was being considered for the national team. Back then, when you were crying with colic in your crib, the country was going through some difficult times, and the worst thing was the noise. It was understandable – we were in the middle of a war, there was the issue of taking charge, we were on the path to independence, nobody was supporting us, all that was left was to shout, which we're quite good at; when we ask for something as a nation, we always shout. Or we shout for the sake of shouting. Like this," he put the chessboard down from his lap and, opening his toothless mouth, shouted, "A-a-a-a-a-a-a-a-a-a-a-a-a-a-a-a-a-a-a-a-a-a-a-a-a-a-a-a-a..."

The lemon-colored park shuddered.

The old man used the tortured handkerchief to wipe the milky bubbles that had appeared on his lips. He laughed without opening his mouth, the way cats laugh.

"You see? Everyone was terrified, for some reason. The statue went pale. But, back then, this was an inseparable part of life. You hear the way I'm talking to you now? Back them, noise was like speech, and we had grown used to it and, especially when we were sitting in parks, we would play under the booms of the protestors, and we would play well. Believe me, we Armenians are no worse than the Indians or Arabs; if the old guys get together one day and go to Calcutta to take part in the street tournament, we will win because we know how to concentrate when it's noisy, how to transform the noise into silence, and move. And on one of those days when we were gathered in the park to watch the game between Husik the Electrician and Smbat, something happened.

During the endgame, Husik moved his rook and began to pluck the hairs off his head with his half-burnt fingers. At the same time, a child that had stuck his head through the mass of sweaty and hairy men, whispered,

"Wrong move."

Everyone turned around. The boy was embarrassed. He pressed harder on a wooden chessboard under his arm. It was an awkward moment. The kings of street chess had all been standing there – they had come from Kond, Komitas, Bangladesh, Yerrord Mas, Sari Tagh – and the king of kings Husik the Electrician was sitting at the table, the very man whose name resounded throughout the city. He would roll up the sleeves of his shirt in both summer and winter, and when his opponent made a move, he would always say, three times, "Hmm, hmm, hmm..."

He would fill one of his pockets with sunflower seeds and put his tools in the other. Husik was an extraordinary man – may God bless his soul a thousand times – he liked vodka made from cornelian cherry, and when he went to someone's house to work on their electric lines, he would take his chessboard along. After finishing the job, we would always ask for a shot of vodka and, after finishing it, he would set up the chessboard and challenge the man of the house to a game. And woe be to anyone who would try to refuse, a fight would always break out. Husik had done some time at the police station for such brawls, but he would use these as opportunities to play chess with the policemen on duty there. The only person that Husik would teach was his wife.

They said that before going to sleep Husik would use water colors to paint a chessboard on his wife's naked body. Her delicate skin would grow wavy with each breath, the chess board rocking like a little boat, which acted like a special effect for each move being made.

"Husik the Electrician had been a self-taught player and he boasted that he had been able to quickly and correctly arrange a chessboard at the age of seven months. It isn't very likely, but perhaps that's the way it was. He would play with fifteen people at once and, on some occasions, he would make a move, then leave to fix some damaged cables, only to come back in the second half of the day to continue the game. But the most important and significant day in his life was when he met Tigran Petrosyan – he told everybody about it and lit one cigarette after the other because he was so emotional. There were cases when Husik was seen sitting with kids, telling them in all seriousness about how he had once played a tied game with the world champion and been at the receiving end of the man's praise. Husik expressed pride at the fact that he had, on one occasion, sent the champion *tolma* grape leaves by helicopter.

He dreamed that, when he died, his body would be placed in a large box shaped like a chessboard, closed tightly with two silver-plated locks, and then buried. I'm telling you all this so that you get an idea of what a character he was. The King of the Streets. By the way, he was also a serious *khash* eater. And for a scrawny kid to question a move made by a man like that? It was a joke.

Husik began to boil.

"What do you mean, 'wrong move'?"

"You're going to lose in several moves," the boy continued.

Husik lost his cool, and raised his body, which had been bent carefully like a folding bed, pointing his awkward hand in the boy's direction.

"I'm not going to continue the game until this whelp leaves."

Everyone intervened, trying to persuade him not to take offense. The boy's words should not be taken seriously, they said, but a voice then rang out.

"Can I continue the game in Smbat's place?"

That was already too much. Husik exploded.

"You… you… Come on, then, hurry up and sit down… Sit down! Let's see what you can do…"

And that was the end, the end of a champion, because a short while later, the boy brought Husik's sweaty king to his knees with a stunning offensive.

Freedom Square was bursting with noise, our nation was shouting loudly, and in that incessant commotion, a funereal silence had descended on the park across the street, an intrauterine silence, and it was in this silence that we were seeing off our invincible king and declaring an unknown, ten-year-old kid our new monarch.

"Give me a cigarette," the old man lit the slim with teary eyes, filled his lungs with the smoke, launched a ball of spit on the ground and then blurred it with his shoe. "I have no regrets that the guys and I did not participate in the protests during those years of the war, that we were busy with some very important work – playing chess. Our life was our game, with no blood or bullets, no killing or rape, no kebabs or heroes, with only the acme as our objective. We were on the side of a mental struggle – searching for the right move with closed eyes, concentrated thought. This brought together taxi drivers, electricians, drywall laborers, and retired teachers, all of whom had big brains. But we were neglected, insulted, and jeered; like Odo of Sully, they banned chess and told us that it is a loafer's pastime, that we should go to the battlefield and fire guns, it was wrong to spend the whole day seated in front of a piece of wood. But let me continue."

The newly-crowned king lived in the Kond district. He was a strange child, with a phlegmatic smile constantly on his face. Experts said that a new chess star was born, some had their reservations and thought that his talent would fade with age, but time showed that the child kept improving. When white milk mixed with black mud, the champion would close his eyes and leave the game, the people, the hall, himself, and everyday life; he would go to listen to the next move. Look at how this bluish smoke rises – it is straight at first, then cylindrical, it breaks up and turns in circles like a pair of tango dancers in an embrace, spinning, spinning as it dissipates and disappears, with only a fog to betray the fact that it had existed. You saw the smoke a moment ago, right? That was how you would see the champion one moment, and then you would not. He would disappear inside himself, flying beyond space and time with indescribable concentration. But then he would suddenly wake up in the middle of the game and start an unpredictable combination of moves, launch a barrage of attacks, and take many of his opponents' pieces. The person at the other end would be unable to calculate any real options and would soon find his king facing an untimely demise.

He won against all the grandmasters.

Few people in our city knew about him – just the tiny intelligentsia that you would come across in the cheapest of cafés, near newspaper kiosks, and bookstores; they would talk about him in whispers to each other. They were embarrassed. I grew close to the young king's father and one day he talked to me on a bus stop about his son's inexplicable behavior.

The father said that the champion had a strange way of life, he did not talk to anyone, rejected any food with meat in it, sat motionless all evening in front of a chessboard, and appeared the next morning in the same position, with a smile on his face. He would drink coffee and eat semi-sweet biscuits made by a baker they knew and shaped like chess pieces. He would be careful when eating them, trying to avoid losing any crumbs. That old baker, who had the figure of the knight on a chessboard, was his only guest and playmate in those final years; like someone who had lost his tongue, he would knock on the door and stand quietly on the threshold with the box of biscuits in his hand, then skip and hop to the champion's room. They would play a game but without a chessboard or pieces. For one hundred ninety-one days, the champion had not said a word. At first, they thought there was a problem with his tongue or vocal chords, but the doctor could not find a single symptom, constantly taking notes with his pencil. On one occasion, the father noticed that his son was deep in thought over the Nimzowitsch Defence.

He was very worried.

The old man grew quiet. He rubbed the fogged lenses of his glasses with his handkerchief, you could see men walking on the moon with glasses like those.

There was silence in Saryan Park.

"You're tired of hearing all this, I know, but be patient, there isn't much left," he said and continued, "It was a Saturday and the king had received a call from the President's staff and was told to be at the reception of the Presidential Palace at eight that evening. The boy was wearing a striped blazer.

When he walked into the office, the President was nowhere to be seen. The champion walked. Soon, the muscles of his legs grew tired. He slung the blazer over his shoulders. He stopped to take a break. Then he continued to walk. He was sweating. A black spot appeared in the distance. The head of state came into view. The boy's white teeth glistened. The President looked taller on television. He swayed as he walked closer, then said hello with a yellow, withered hand and indicated his chessboard with unblinking eyes. The ivory pieces eagerly awaited their commanders. They sat down. The game was started.

It turned out to be a tense game. The head of state was well prepared. His moves were logical and careful; at first, thanks to his experience, he was able to exert his will on the pieces, but that did not last long. In the middle of the battle, the President lost control and his concentration wavered, he made one mistake after the other, his moves became pointless, he grew confused in his lack of resolution, and led himself to a dead end. The king was toying with him – he could have ended the game at any moment, but he was gaining sincere pleasure at the President's exclamations of helplessness.

The game ended in a draw, although it would have been better for the boy to win. The President went completely pale, realizing that the boy had done this on purpose. He tried to smile but failed. He felt ashamed.

"Bobby once said that if he played against God, it would end in a draw… I ask you not to tell anyone about this," the President wanted to stare outside, but the room did not have a window… "People start to resemble chess pieces, they don't believe me…" "In India, the *rajas* spent more time mentally watching chess players, they would sit at a chessboard with much less frequency; I cannot stop myself from playing, it is beyond my powers," he continued, "I can't.." "My mother taught me to play chess…" The President's wrinkly face dried with sorrow.

They said a wordless goodbye to each other.

The king was smiling.

On the last day, they saw him in a café, sitting with a stranger.

The phone rang unexpectedly, he answered the call.

"Hi, how are you? It's God. I like beer. Let's meet today on Tumanyan Street, I'll buy you one and we can talk."

God had a handsome face and even a leather wallet. He greeted the boy with respect, complimented the plump waitress and eagerly ordered beer.

"You know, I'm sad, very sad. I feel lonely.

"I am unable to find a way out of my own game. Down here, they've forgotten about me. I find myself unable to tell their faces apart, I only hear sounds of pleading and crying. I'm losing my mind because of these sounds, I need silence; you have to understand, my throat has dried up. I'm tired of champions' laurels. I've beaten all the chess players in heaven and hell – seriously, in all honesty – even though I have to say the team from Hell was not bad. But you are invading my thoughts, your silence gives me no peace… I need it… You have tried to listen in on my oves. To be honest, I wanted to forget about you. I was given reports every day about an Armenian king that lived on the Earth, an invicible chess champion that had given up on the spoken word… Forgive me, but I could not remove that from my thoughts, you did not allow it. A suspicion took hold of me, I suspected… That's why I'm here. I'm asking you to play a game with me, one game…"

God grew emotional.

Tense with the expectation of a response, he took a large gulp of beer, ate a salty breadstick, exhaled loudly, and continued,

"Well, everything has been set up there, they're expecting us. 1440 grams against the Universe. Accept the challenge, make your move, such a contest has never taken place before…"

From afar, they saw him staring at the sky for a long time, tears running down his face.

The boy was turning into a transparent cloud.

Everyone was feathery there.

The boy with the striped blazer walked forward, his hands in his pockets.

A majestic chessboard appeared in the clouds.

God walked towards him.

He said happily, in a loud voice,

"Make way! The king approaches…"

TRANSPARENT BOTTLES

Why do people drink vodka?
They drink to make all the children of the world cry.
They drink to snack on pickles.
They drink to remember the dead and God.
They drink to drink.
They drink to kill people.
They drink to love.
They drink to be violent.
They drink to forget.
They drink to live.

Father drinks because he can't help drinking.

My mother crushes a pill into the soup. The movements of her wrist are swift and agile. Now my father will exit the bathroom, whistling, and with hands trembling hungrily, he will try the chicken soup where the secret that mother and I share has dissolved. I can't swallow my food. He quickly finishes his soup, drinks a glass of ice water, goes to his room. I think, maybe he is going to die, the pill will affect his blood circulation and his heart will explode. I feel sorry for him. Minutes pass. My father is uneasy. He rises from his bed and hurries to an open window; he's short of breath. He's gasping for air. He doesn't know why he feels like this. There is fear in his eyes, the same kind of fear I had seen in the eyes of a street dog gnawing at a bone. My mother and I sit in the kitchen with the silent patience of murderers. Father starts howling. We run to his side, lay him down to bed. The sheets stink of alcohol, his heart is throbbing in his chest.

The pill is starting to affect him. We were warned that the patient will feel dizziness, panic, nausea, an accelerated heart rate, a sense of emptiness, disgust toward alcohol. My mother made me her accomplice for her own benefit, it will be easier on her when she remembers that as she was crushing the pill into his soup, I was next to her. The next day, I can't stand it anymore. I ask mother to stop. I only hear the constant clanking of the spoon. I take the merciless plate and smash it against the wall. Enough.

There are a few days left until New Year. The pork roast is ready to be served. I open the apartment door. I call out, but no one answers. Nobody is at home. I enter my parents' bedroom. My father is standing with his back to me. He can't sense my presence. He's drinking vodka straight from a 20-liter bottle. I stand motionless. He turns around and is instantly drunk the moment he sees me. He tears up. Don't tell your mother, please. Whatever you want, I'll buy it.

I have just started the fifth grade at school, I steal books from my grandpa's library and wait for my father to keep his promise.

On the first of January he comes home carrying a huge music system. A bribe for my silence. It feels like the audio system stinks of vodka, garlic, and the deceit that burns me from the inside. I secretly give my father a glass of vodka every day, that's why he loves me more than anyone else in the family. He is grateful.

We have a summer house. Father built it. It's the only place where I feel like a human being, he says. On our way there we stop at a small shop constructed of wood, where the saleswoman, without any questions, hands us a cola and a bottle of vodka. I play in the garden, I enjoy my drink and I know that in the kitchen, father is having a glass of vodka once every ten minutes. He thinks I'm not aware of this, but I'm sure, in some corner of his heart he knows that I know, and he is using me, but that's okay, let him do it. Until he drinks and finishes a full bottle, I maintain the ten-minute intervals without missing a beat. I want to make sure I don't interrupt him. We return home hugging each other like two people in love, we are covered in mud and scratches. Mother hits my father, calls me greedy and filthy; an animal who has sold himself for a bottle of cola. My father falls into bed. No one enters the room. He is alone. Mother sleeps next to my sister. I enter the room in the middle of the night, there is no air, the walls are breathing alcohol. He is still in the same position, with his clothes on, curled up like a fetus. I want to hear him snoring, to make sure he isn't dead. There is no sound. Trembling, I gently press my fingers to his forehead, his veins are bursting. He's alive, he hasn't died. I feel a little sad; if he died at least it would give him some respite. My ears ring with the deafening sound of shattering bottles and my father's eyes, fogged with gloom. I smash his bottles of vodka one after another. Then I sit down, wash my eyes with water and leave. I knock on the neighbor's door. I tell him that I scratched my leg on a dried tree branch and ask for a glass of vodka and a cotton ball to disinfect the wound. My neighbor gives me a glass of rubbing alcohol, a cotton ball and with good intentions, wishes me luck. Without watering down the rubbing alcohol, I give it to my father and help him drink it. Almost unconsciously he tries to thank me but doesn't succeed. I can feel it.

The director of the department at the drug rehabilitation hospital continually shakes his head. He tries to light the red pipe in his mouth, but fails. He tries to listen to me. I tell him that my father is a famous surgeon and I want to save him, cure him, help him somehow, but I don't want people to know about it. He understands and shares my concern, he lights the pipe again, but it stubbornly refuses to be lit up. He explains that the hospital rooms are a paid service, and there are strict rules. Nurses are intolerant. Every day they give a glass of vodka to their patients and that's it, if they don't obey, the nurses put them in straitjackets and tie them to their beds. But what if he dies, I say. A lot of people die here, I have nothing to hide on that front, you understand that at the end of the day, this can't be cured, he says. I don't want father to die. I will miss him.

The walls are red. My father has fallen to the floor. Blood gushes from his torn temple. The liquid endlessly shoots out. It is beautiful. Reminiscent of the fountains in Republic Square. My mother and sister are at home, in their rooms. I put my finger into the wound. The blood is watery, like our local fruit juice. I clean the wound with iodine. I wash his face with a kitchen rag, I bandage the wound; he taught me how to do that. Father, father I hate you. You lie. He laughs. Where did you fall? Near the railway. No one saw you, I say hopefully. All the neighbors saw it. A kid helped me and brought me home. I'm sorry.

From his underwear, he takes out a crumpled thousand-dram banknote. Take this, treat your girlfriend to a cup of coffee. I put him to bed.

Sleep.

I go to a priest. He suggests that I take part in the liturgy. The Lord hears everything. His answer is silence. Yes, he only silently condoles with you. I don't need his pity. I am upset. They give me clothes, candles and incense.

The ceremony is lengthy. The priest approaches me after the liturgy, puts his hand on my shoulder in a friendly manner. You should trust in God, his heart is big, he will show you the way. I don't know how Jesus would have felt if his father was an alcoholic. I tell the priest that I feel sorry for my father, I want him to die, but I don't want him to go to hell, that's where he is now. I feel ashamed, I say. Don't be ashamed, my son, you are not alone in this. He calms me down and says a friendly farewell.

I dream of transparent bottles. My father is sitting in all these bottles. He asks for help. I can't hear his voice. I read his lips. I madly seize the bottles, grab hold of my father's hair, take him out of the bottles, and then cut his head with scissors. I cut through it softly like butter. Then I get the rest of the bottles, take out my fathers, and cut their heads. Great, go on, save me. I offer myself condolences for having a father like you. I squash the talking heads with my feet. There is no blood. Father has no blood. Only water.

My phone rings.

The call is from the hospital.

I leave Masha and hurry out. My heart is fluttering like a dying fish on dry ground. The shards from the shattered bottles in the room have sharp edges, like shark teeth. Father is stark naked. His lower lip is torn in several places. His face looks like a piece of pink meat freshly taken out of the fridge. He doesn't realize that I am next to him. He holds a lighter in his scratched fingers and has stuck it into his nostril, breathing in the gas. His fingers are like clamps. I can't take the lighter out of his hand. I bite his hand. He doesn't feel pain, but reflexively releases his hand. I throw the lighter away, close the door. I tighten my chin like a bulldog, but the scream finds its way out of my lips. I squeal. I want to scream silently in my mind. It seems like I succeed. Only I can hear it.

I find his underwear from under the armchair; I carefully put it on him, followed by the rest – socks, pants, and shirt. Father is ready to go. Please, pull yourself together. I don't want anyone to see me, I try to get this through to him. They won't see you. I hold him tightly at his waist, put his arm over my shoulder. I open the door with fear, I seize a suitable moment and help him out into the corridor. My father looks like a wounded soldier, I drag him forward. Oh my God, please, I hope nobody sees us. A nurse comes out of the X-ray room and walks towards us. We miss each other a lot, I say and try to smile to the nurse, but tears fall from my eyes. The hallway is endless.

Just a few more steps and we will be out of here. My strength deserts me. We fall down. Father falls asleep at once. I am lying over his soft body. My face touches his. My tears are pouring into his eyes, ears and mouth. Their coolness and saltiness sober him up. There is complete silence in the hallway. I pull him to a half-seated position and drag him away. The hallway is endless, like my father's life.

The large black letters spell out a word –
EXIT

I parked my car near the entrance. I place my father next to the driver's seat. I tie him with a rope so he doesn't fall over. Nobody is at home to welcome us. I sit on the edge of the sofa. I feel sleepy.

"I hate you, I am ashamed that you are my father. You don't love me; if you did, you would quit drinking for my sake. There is no love inside you, you only love drinking, you have swallowed me through your bottles. I want to kill you inside myself, I don't want to carry the name you gave me, your last name. Everybody has a dead person inside and you are the one inside me, Father".

I go to work with an empty heart.

I wait for my phone to ring.

Where has Father fallen this time? At his workplace? In the room? In the yard, in the toilet, in the bushes?

Father has fallen down.

He is alone.

They locked him in the room, he is bleeding and can't call for help.

I need to hurry.

I rush to him. He is in the garage. With a bottle of petrol and a rubber hose next to him.

He was inhaling it.

There are punctures from injections on his wrists.

It's terrifying!

I am standing on the blocks of Cascade. There is a light breeze. There is darkness below and the stars above.

The guard of the park is rushing towards me. Get down at once, are you crazy? His voice dulls in the air.

I walk down Babayan Street.

I pass by Chaykoff store, where I usually buy tea for my girlfriend.
I run home.
I run because I am afraid.
I run because I don't want to see transparent bottles.
I run because all the children of the world run along with me.
I run because I don't want things to be this way.
I run because I should secretly give him a glass of vodka.
I run because he's waiting for me.

BIRDS

Birds fly and they don't,
Birds fall and they fly
Giacomo Leopardi

"The most important day of my life… The doctor was saying, 'You'll feel a sharp pain, then shock, and that's it, a very, very powerful pain…' It's okay, I'll bear it for a moment… my head will explode… mother will be very worried; as soon as they tell her, she might faint, she won't believe it… Then she'll be in the hospital for a few months… Maybe she'll even end up committing suicide…"

"Black… Black…"

"What?"

"Black…"

"Where are you, Piglet?"

"Sorry to bother you… do you have any chocolate? I'm hungry…"

The weak fluttering of Piglet's arms could be heard. He landed softly on the floor, put on his slippers and walked up to Black's bed…

Black took out a chocolate from the box and held it out to the boy…

"Here… see… Brittle, Squirrel, take them all, my family had brought these over…

"I know, I'd seen them, snort, snort," Piglet smiled cunningly, grabbed the chocolates with fingers that were trembling hungrily and opened them, taking turns to stuff them in his mouth. His massive cheeks were fluttering in delight. After turning the chocolates into a paste in his mouth, he swallowed them regretfully, then swept his large tongue across his teeth to pick the pieces that had lodged themselves in between. Soon, his restless sound once again stood out among the snoring…

"Black… What am I going to do? I'm the one on duty tomorrow and the Commander ordered that this place must be clean… He pulled at this and a few feathers came out. He said that if I don't do it, he'll drive that stick into my ass…"

Piglet started to cry…

"Come on, why are you whining like a woman? Don't worry, we'll think of something…"

"What? How? Oh God, if this place isn't clean tomorrow, the Commander will kill me…"

His voice was absorbed by a bleat emitted by one of the sleeping soldiers.

"Sounds like there's a cow chasing him," Piglet whispered with a serious look on his face…

"What a time the President picked to come. They're demanding one hundred percent cleanliness for his visit…"

"What are we going to do? Snort, snort…"

Piglet took his gigantic head into his hands…

"Don't worry. We'll bring Davit over in the morning, he'll clean it up…"

"We can't do that, he's been taken to the defense post…"

"We'll call Beak… Don't you worry… we'll think of something…"

"It won't… it won't work," Piglet said in desperation, "Beak already has a supporter, he gives a monthly salary…"

"That's not good… Ah yes, we've forgotten about Bibik. Bibik from the first regiment…"

"Bibik won't do any cleaning… he doesn't do any work anymore, they've hurt his feelings…"

"Leave the convincing to me… he won't turn me down. I'll trick him somehow into agreeing, it'll work out, don't worry… You worry about filling your stomach," Black smiled…

Piglet relaxed a little. His childlike face lit up.

"Hey, Black, have you heard? I read that story you mentioned at the library the other day. It took me six days to finish it… *The Snake*… Who wrote it? Stabeck, Stubeck? What was his name again?"

"Steinbeck… Steinbeck. Well? Did you like it?"

"Very much, bro. I mean, I hadn't read anything from the Bible before, but once you told me about it, I got excited and picked it up, read all the way to the end…"

Piglet was growing more relaxed with each word.

"Ok then, go get some rest. When the morning comes, everything will be fine…"

"Good night…"

"Good night."

* * *

Bibik was smoking, his wings spread against the cafeteria wall. He was examining the movement of the wisps of cigarette smoke, alternatively between talking to himself, sobbing and laughing. Bibik was a pretty boy, with blue eyes, a girlish, delicate torso, wandering eyes…

"Hey, Bib. How are you? What's going on?"

Black skipped towards Bibik with careful steps and stopped at a distance of four meters…

"I'm good, thanks. How are you? What's going on at your end?"

"Good, nothing much. Our regiment commander is on our case again…"

Bibik hung his head…

"Black, come on. I know you're here for a reason. Spill it, what's on your mind?"

"Well, you've probably heard, Bib, that the President is coming… In a word, we need you… that space… you know… needs to be cleaned. It was assigned to Piglet, but if it isn't clean before the President's visit…"

"I've always helped you, you know that. Have I ever said no? I'd do anything for you, but not anymore… not anymore… sorry, I don't want to…"

The blue tears rolled down Bibik's eyes, painting his cheeks…

"Has something happened, Bib? Who's hurt you? Tell me… say something… I'll help you…"

"…"

"…"

"I was sitting at the riverbank reading a letter from my sister the other day. She had sent it a week ago, but there hadn't been any time to read it. I was looking for a hidden place where nobody would see me. I had just opened the envelope when Lieutenant Gege appeared from nowhere and grabbed the letter… then… then he started reading it and laughing, shouting loudly, "Bibik, your sister has lovely handwriting. Persuade her to come here for me, I won't let you out the toilet till you make her come here…"

Bibik was trembling. He had withdrawn. His feathers had stiffened and quivered.

Black froze for a few minutes… Then he strengthened his back with difficulty and walked backwards… He was barely able to keep himself from falling, his head was spinning. He found it difficult to see Bibik, he was in a cloud.

"Please, Bib… I need you. Do the work, please, for my sake…"

"…"

"Black, you know how much I respect you. I'll help you again, but this will be the last time," Bibik barely managed to say…

"You had helped me for the last time a month ago too, Bib… But there are no last times in life…"

* * *

When Bibik showed up there holding a dirty bucket, Piglet seemed to be reborn. He carefully took off his wings and hung them from a nail on the wall, then started to tidy up with the delicate fingers of a pianist. He filled the bucket with the fresh and hardened dirt of the soldiers, the rotten papers and cigarette butts, the bottles of cola… He cleaned the place completely, then swept it meticulously, wetted the floor, and left it tidy and fresh. Black was perched on an electric wire and watched him, after which he filled a plastic bag with chocolates and held it out to Bibik, tied to the end of a tree branch. The boy lit up with happiness and took the bag, opened it and put the candy in his pockets…

"Black, do you know what I miss?"

"What?"

"*Gozinaki*, mother would send me some from time to time…"

Bibik lit a cigarette and continued,

"I heard that you're reading books, Black…"

"You heard right…"

"What are you reading?"

"Various things… I don't know…"

"I like reading too… I wanted to go to the library the other day, I was planning to read Steinbeck's *The Snake*. I'd read all of the other stuff by him that we have here in the city, but not *The Snake*. The librarian wouldn't let me in. She said that if the soldiers saw that I was touching the books, they would no longer enter the library… Well, I'm off, take care." Bibik took off his wings from the nail on the wall, fastened them to his back and flew off, immediately blending in with the swallows spinning in the air…

* * *

It was a stressful day. The President came but he did not end up staying long because it was raining sorrowfully, wetting his shoes. The commander was satisfied with the cleanness of the space. Piglet was mad with joy. He had flown down to the village and come back with curds, *lavash* bread, and vodka, preparing a little feast in Black's honor.

"Black, thank you, snort snort, thank you, snort, for everything… I would be lost without you… thank you, brother," as he stood there with a glass in his hand, Piglet looked like Botero's Roman Warrior.

The toasts continued with brief intervals. Black was quiet. He was drinking without eating, he kept sighing deeply, constantly brushing the feathers of the wings stretched over the bed.

"I felt really sorry for Bibik, Piglet… He should at least commit suicide…"

"Bibik? Why? Why should anyone feel sorry for toilet-cleaning animals? And anyway, animals don't have souls… snort, snort, snort, snort…"

Black flew up and struck out with his wing, overturning the table. His facial muscles were twitching in waves…

"Get up… Get up, I say… quickly… Move your ass, hurry… I'm talking to you… Fly off and go to sleep… I want to see you asleep in ten minutes, understood? Do you understand what I'm saying?"

The walls of the military compound shook with Black's shouting…

Piglet, startled, did not even manage to bite the cucumber he was holding. He quickly disappeared into the darkness, mumbling incoherently to himself…

Black was unable to sleep that night. He put on his wings and flew out the window.

* * *

In the morning, after breakfast, Black went to the library, picked up a worn copy of the magazine *Spring*, and started reading *The Snake*. He had just started to sink into the story when Piglet came in through the door, his face twisted.

"Black… Black… snort, have you heard the news? Leiutenant Gege has been found dead near the river. They say that, before he was killed, his face was doused in petrol and burned…"

"What do I care? How many times have I told you not to bother me when I'm reading…"

Piglet hung his head.

"I'm sorry, Black…"

He turned around and was already leaving when Black shouted after him…

"Piglet…"

The boy turned.

"Goodbye, Piglet…"

"…"

"Goodbye, Black," Piglet, surprised, exclaimed happily and flew out the half-open door…

Black continued reading the story.

MY RETURN

* * *

A piece of paper was stuck to the polished stone of the church – "Please turn off your cellphones when you enter." Why did I kill you? I turn off my phone. I enter. I'm sweating…

Mass is being celebrated. The priest is singing, but almost to himself, nothing can be heard. There are many people in the church. They've come to you, they are asking you, begging, threatening, they have locked tight the doors of their souls before coming. Why are they scared of you in your own home? They don't dare spit in your face…

I don't believe in God but, for some reason, I am convinced that he believes in me. I can't look him in the eyes, but his sad face gives me no peace. It would have been good if he could forget, if he could look past my presence. In the icon, Jesus' face grows gloomier. For a moment, I think that the person praying next to me is a murderer, the one next to him a thief, the third one a madman, the fourth an ape-like creature, the fifth an old witch… Hee hee hee hee hee hee hee… Jesus cackles like a devil. That's you! You! You are those things… hee hee hee hee hee… I pray to the Lord asking for at least a few thousand drams during the week so that I can buy a book. He smiles, perhaps he hasn't heard such a strange prayer in a long time. I make him happy…

I want to buy the Turkish writer Orhan Pamuk's *Istanbul* using the money sent by the Savior. It's a strange desire, presented as a prayer. I am a bit embarrassed but I put on a straight face and ask one more time, "If you give me the book, I'll come again to you. If you don't, I won't return, okay?" Forgive me, will you? Okay, bye…

I walk out. It has started to rain, his heart is overcome with emotion…

* * *

I hear a dog. It looks like it was careless and has ended up being hit by a car. It is lying in the middle of the street, its skull crushed, mouth open, guts lying everywhere. Cars keep driving over it again and again, squishing the remains of its organs. I buy a bag of apples and enjoy them, looking all day at the ripped tissues of the dog. When the day grows dark, its organs, fur, and limbs have become a minced salad. Then I remember, the wind is blowing and the salad is being spread throughout the street. I feel like I'm going to get a taste of it at any moment, so I feel nauseated. I drop my hand into my bag and walk away…

* * *

I open the garage door and pull off the sheet. We embrace. I kiss its steering wheel and leather seats, the smell of the inside fills my lungs. Inside, I find half a bottle of Campari and pour its contents down my throat. I start the engine… forward… I have missed the city so much. I drive the streets of the city day and night. I go into the Malkhas jazz club, have whiskey until I'm close to blacking out. I step outside. I call a guy I know and remind him of his debt, I tell him that if he does not pay up, I will use a cup to kill Herman. A few hours later, he brings the money and apologizes, saying honestly that he had lost all hope of seeing me. I don't let him leave. Nobody should simply leave like that in life. We go into Cub and have a mojito each. Then he probably leaves, while I get into my car and continue. We are above the ground, at the level of the building rooftops. We go along the electric power lines. I stand over the sea, coming down and taking a seat among the waves…

* * *

The night was as long as eternity. There was nothing to drink, I was forced to smoke. My mother had left pomegranates on the table. I picked one up and, smacking my lips like a predator, started to eat. I remember my father, who was a hard drinker. I read and say,

"Here's to you, Dad…" My teeth sink into the skin… I'm eating pomegranates in honor of your toast…

ARAM PACHYAN

We go through the chambers of the city's heart, narrow and broad, veins that are long and short. Where should I go? A club, a strip bar? My heart peeks through the bars of its cage, waiting for a truck that I can hit and turn into little stars, to destroy my car and myself, ending up on the curb. I stop in front of the Melody café, step outside and have a beer. My body wants nudity. I haven't been loved in such a long time. I've missed feeling the weightless body of a woman…

* * *

Leningradyan Avenue is the same. I slow down the car and move closer to the curb. She's a petite girl, she sits in the car and says, holding her breath, "You've probably forgotten the Gates of Heaven, drive and I'll show you the way." You can tell that she's practicing a lot at home, but the words still don't come out smoothly and there is too much theatrical emotion in them.

We go to Hotel Sam, I ask for a room. As soon as we're inside, she starts rushing to take off her clothes.

"Don't hurry," I say, kissing her shoulder…

"I don't have time. You might have nothing to do, but every minute counts in my case…"

"I have returned…"

We light a cigarette…

"What's your name?"

"Veronica…"

"Did you make that up?"

"It doesn't matter…"

"I've made up my name too…"

We are so alike… Veronica… Vera… Ver… You know, my love for you is as big as the world in which we live…

I caress her waist with my long fingers, the depressions in her pelvis…

"How old are you?"

"Seventeen…"

I think, "Ah, you crazy girl. You're dearer to me than all the Mariams, this I know…"

"I have returned."

"Yes, I got that. Where from?"

"…"

"Are you all right?"

"Forget about it."

I kiss your shoulderblade, trying to touch your skin lightly with my tongue, thinking that this will make you feel good. I hug your thighs, we lie in the bed… Your face and delicate body have been worn out from your whoring. You have hung a cross from your white neck. It's Jesus' crucified body, engraved. My delicate, emotional little girl, I believe in the cross that hangs silently on your skin… Your naked body, slender, covered in goosebumps, white, worthy of worship… Little girl, there are the traces of a scalpel below your abdomen…

"Do you have a child?"

"Yes, I do. Let me show you a picture of my little beauty…"

She takes out a crumpled photograph from her bag, and an angel sitting on a swing looks out at us with wet blue eyes…

"Shall we get dressed?

"What? What is the meaning of this? Don't you want to…"

"I can't, I'm sorry… It won't work out…"

I kiss your hot neck, rubbing my cheek against yours.

"Have you had a lot to drink?"

"No…"

"Don't worry about it, I'll help you out…"

"It won't work out…"

"Are you impotent?"

"I don't know… maybe… I don't know…"

I slowly put on your clothes… I give you all the money I have and *Istanbul*…

You don't take the book, you are honest enough to take only the money…

"That's just too bad…"

Deep down, you feel sorry for me, like I do for you…

"Don't worry about it. Buy the kid a toy…"

You leave, a sweet look of disdain on your face. We are left alone in the room, alone within ourselves… I lie down on the side of the bed where the girl had been, kissing her sad lips, embracing her. I embrace my return.

TORONTO

Whenever my father upset my mother, I would always go to Toronto, where there was an old worn bed with a metal frame placed on top of beehives, and by its headboard, a bookshelf that practically reached the sky, filled with countless books. In Toronto, I would sit on the biggest mushroom that had grown between the floorboards and look at the waves of the three long hairs that fell from my grandpa's bald head, which shivered from the hot steam rising from the cup of tea in his hand. "Now we will drink tea and eat *lokhum* together," my grandfather would say, patting my head. "Don't worry, everything will be fine." "I don't want to, Grandpa. Tell me about your bees," I would say. "In Toronto, the bees know how to talk like people. They can also sing, recite poems, they help and heal each other, they learn foreign languages... You believe me, don't you?" he'd ask, setting his teacup down on the table. "Yes, Grandpa, I believe you. But the bees in our hives, why don't they talk?" "Ehhhh, my child, they don't listen to our bees. And when nobody listens to them, the bees get upset and never speak again. They choose silence and hard work." "Where are we now, Grandpa?" I would ask him again and again. "We're in the forest, and in the heart of the forest lies Toronto. I'll show you."

My grandfather would lean his body on his cane and stand up. He would pull the thickest, largest book off the bookshelf and open it from the middle. "Come close, my child, closer..." With bated breath, I would approach my grandfather and hug his leg, which rattled like a train. I would look at his hand. From between the pages, my grandfather would take out a huge leaf, a lush, green leaf that made rustling noises. "Do you see? Look carefully. Here is Toronto." His glazed eyes would light up the entire surface of the leaf. Tears would pool in the whites of his eyes. "Give me your hand. Come on now, your hand." Slowly and a little timidly, I would slowly extend my hand to the stem of the leaf and hold it. "Good... hold it tightly, my child.

Do not be afraid. When your father slaps your mother, Toronto gets drawn on her cheek. Come, kiss the leaf. The pain will go away. Toronto will heal the pain." Then, with his faint voice like a breeze blowing through a fir tree, he would add, "When you are sad, remember that you are not alone. Toronto is always with you. At night, if you can't sleep, repeat 50 times in your head: Toronto, Toronto, Toronto… until your eyes close and the Seneca float by you in their canoes, and like snowflakes, the birds of the forest come and rest on your shoulders, the angels on bicycles, the roosters with carts, the tiny donkeys, no bigger than grains of sand, sitting on the streetcars, and finally, the talking bees, who will sing the sweetest song for you and recite the most profound poetry. They will become your closest friends…"

As my grandfather spoke, the mushroom would grow, until my feet were lifted off the ground. Holding the leaf tightly, I would rise, almost reaching the sky, and I would see the highest shelves. When I would look down for a moment, my grandfather would look as small as a bee, his cane happily rejoicing in the air…

Toronto 45

Toronto 46

Toronto 47

The three hairs on his head flutter like a white flag. His tea has probably gone cold.

Toronto 48

The quivering of the cane reminds me of soft twinkles. Now and then, the circular outlines of its knots come into view. I lose him in its ink-coloured layers.

Toronto 49

My eyelids are closing for the last time, like heavy gates.

Toronto 50

I fall asleep…

It's been about a month now that I've been packing my bags. I've taken the biggest suitcase in the house, put it out on the balcony, let it air out in the sun, and changed the old, worn lining. On the left side, near the corner, I've glued the excerpt that I had ripped out from the big encyclopedia when I was in school:

Toronto, city in eastern Canada, provincial capital of Ontario. Pop. 3.1 million (including suburbs, 1984). Port on Lake Ontario. Industrial, financial and cultural center. Two universities. 19th century historical monuments. Founded in the 18th century. Was inhabited by Natives in the 17th century, became a French trade hub in the 18th century, and officially became a city under British rule in 1793 (called York until 1834). 1793-1841, administrative centre of British colonial Upper Canada. 1837-1838, site of rebellion against the British.

I've glued it so that it's the first thing that catches my eye when I open the suitcase. Layer by layer, I stack my underwear, socks, toiletries. I choose my green shirt instead of the grey one. I think in Toronto, they'll like my green shirt and I'll get a job. I pack a few warm clothes, it will get cold at night. I also take one pack of cigarettes, a teacup, a spoon, one loaf of *matnakash* bread, one bag of potatoes, a radio, a few small souvenirs, some medication: Analgin and Valerian extract. You never know, I worry that in Toronto I might get heart palpitations from the excitement. The suitcase is getting stuffed. I change and rearrange the clothes and other articles in it almost every day, early in the morning and late at night. I also want to take my father's winter boots with snakeskin over the toes. As I stroll down the streets of Toronto, I'll slow my step and demonstratively pull up my wide-leg jeans so that everyone can see my boots with their snakeskin toes. Perhaps a chubby lady walking next to me eating a pear will notice my shoes and, pear in mouth, will freeze and exclaim, "Oh my God." The clear-rimmed glasses of the gentleman walking towards me will automatically slide down to the tip of his nose as he exclaims discreetly, "*O mon dieu.*" And finally, I'll hear a hoarse, throaty, familiar voice in Armenian, "*Vakh, hors arev…*" But unfortunately the shoes are too big. I would have to leave out a few very valuable things because of them. So I'll have to go in my running shoes.

She is sprinkling the low shrubs of a houseplant with a watering can and scrutinizing me through the corner of her eye. "You're the one who submitted the application, right?" "Yes, I am." "Do you have a specific reason for applying, or…" "I'm going to Toronto." "Toronto? What could you possibly be looking for in Canada… Are you going to sightsee?" "No… I'm going… I want to live there…"

She sits on her office chair, takes some papers out of the drawer… "Live? How? Do you have family there? Sign here." "No, I don't have any family there." "Sign under this paragraph too… Then how are you going? What are you going to do?" "Nothing. At least I'll be close to Gould's chair ." "Sign here too… What do you mean, nothing? Nobody goes to Toron-

to just like that. Try to sign in the right place or we'll have to start over."
"There's no particular reason to go to Toronto." "Just a minute…" She takes
a new sheet of paper from the drawer, sort of like a ticket. "Sign here too…
Hey, do you want a coffee? I've only had one cup today. Don't have a free
second with this damn job." "No, thank you." "Sign here too. Ah, no, no, a
little lower… there you go. Why are your hands shaking?" "I don't know."
"Okay, done. You're free to go. Happy travels to you and good luck. You
know, you've got it right. If my husband agreed, we'd leave today… Have
you said goodbye to your coworkers? I bet they're jealous." "Yeah, we got
together yesterday, we sat, had champagne, I said goodbye to everybody. You
be well, too. Try to get out of this hellhole as soon as possible. Bye." "Thanks,
bye. Have a safe flight." "Thank you."

The envelope is yellowed and torn. I bought it three years ago. I remember well, it was March 2, 2003. The weather was warming up. I walked
towards the booth at the sports school and bought the envelope for 120
drams. At first I put it in my trouser pocket, but I got anxious and afraid
that the edges would get wrinkled in the narrow space. I walked between
the five-storey buildings, stopped in a hidden spot and took out the envelope. At that moment, a man passed by me. He was wearing a white coat,
probably a butcher or a dentist. I immediately hid the envelope so that he
wouldn't see it. Once he had gone quite a distance, he turned into the third
entrance. I quickly took out the envelope and put it in the wide and deep
breast pocket of my jacket. At home, I wrote in thick red pencil on the face
of the envelope: Toronto (ticket money).

For three years, the envelope would be in a constant state of flux, swelling and draining. It would appear in all the likely and unlikely corners of
the house: in drawers, in pillowcases, under the loose parquet tiles, even in
the crack in the elevator ceiling. Toronto (ticket money), all that's visible
now is the last part in brackets. Mind you, the money is the important
part – 15,600 drams. I pick up the old envelope and put it in my suitcase,
cramming it between the pack of cigarettes and the teacup, so that it won't
fall out if it's moved around. It's the last day. Tomorrow it'll all be over.
Tomorrow I won't be here. Just a few hours, and that's it. I go to bed. I lay
my head on the pillow.

Toronto 16

Toronto 17

Toronto 18

The light goes on in the room. "Get up, get dressed. Your dad hasn't come home." My mother's polka-dotted nightgown flows loosely away from her body. Half of her pale chest is looking at me mournfully. She hasn't even noticed that she's wearing her nightgown, that she ever put it on in the first place, that half of her breast, with its stretched nipple, is showing. My father is gone. He's always gone. He shows up once in a while around noon, like a dead man's ghost, betraying his presence in our lives. He shows up to say that he is miserable. I don't believe him. I scare him. I tell him that if he keeps it up, I'll leave home, that I'll go to Toronto and never come back, that he'll be left alone. He doesn't believe me, and doesn't even hear my voice anymore because he's not in the room, he's gone away. He has appeared just to disappear. Now it's my turn. I'm going to hunt him down, going to set my trap, sharpen my vision, my hearing, keep my hand on the trigger without trembling, without doubt, without fear. I go everywhere, through wide and narrow streets. I go to the hospital, leave the hospital. I walk down the roads that have been the only roads of my life. I return down the roads that have been the only roads of my life. I go to the morgue, I go home, I go to the summer house, I go to the hospital… I come and I go, just as the power would during the years of the blockade. I come and I go, like the seasons of the year, like a shameless cat. He is not here, not anywhere. I start to think, maybe he never was, but there's not time to think. Thoughts are like those familiar roads to me, where I come and go…

It's time.

That's it, just a few moments and…

I can barely lift the suitcase off the ground. I've added new things, in particular my notebooks filled with draft copies and finally, after giving it a lot of thought, I've decided to take my father's worn boots. They'll just look so good.

It's quiet and dark outside.

I turn the key twice. The cellar door creaks open. A muddle of smells hits my face. I go inside. It's a tight space. My suitcase barely fits. I somehow manage to set it down next to the preserves. I flip over the box that's meant for winter pickles, sit on it, and close the door.

The plane still has a long way to go before reaching Toronto. I may even order an alcoholic beverage. Everything will be all right now, everything will be great. You lean your head against the cold wall. It's quiet and dark inside. The weather is surely perfect in Toronto, nice and cool. The weightless wind carries the pleasant mist of Lake Ontario and the distinct smell of its moss. You can't sleep. Your grandfather's words come to mind: "…when you can't sleep, repeat 50 times in your head Toronto, Toronto, Toronto… until your eyes close and the Seneca float by you in their canoes, and like snowflakes, the birds of the forest come and rest on your shoulders, the angels on bicycles, the roosters with carts, the tiny donkeys, no bigger than grains of sand, sitting on the streetcars, and finally, the talking bees, who will sing the sweetest song for you and recite the most profound poetry. They will become your closest friends…"

Toronto 47
Toronto 48
Toronto 49
They're knocking on the cellar door…
Toronto 50
Toronto 51
Toronto 52
Toronto 53

TWO LOVE STORIES

THE SUITCASE

Suitcases have secrets – the clothes and items piled up inside have their own stories and destinies. I have a thing for old, dusty, abandoned suitcases. I run my hands on the scratches left on their surface over the years and the eight metal cornerpieces, I breathe in the unique smell of the suitcase, the kind of smell that only comes from elderly people, I study for hours the pictures of girls glued to the walls of the suitcase, I take out the soap placed between the folds of mother's nightgown and then put it back. Suitcases are the symbols of leaving and returning.

When my parents would separate twice a day and then get together again, I would always come across suitcases that looked upset. They were tired of being filled and then emptied again. When the moment came to say goodbye, my father would hang his head and stare at my shoes. I wanted to turn back in time, to go inside my father's black suitcase, settle down next to his surgical instruments, examine the bottles of cognac and whiskey, to remain seated in the suitcase as I travel through cities, remember the quietly pronounced names of patients, see the food that he eats, be in the cafés where he drinks brewed beers, differentiate between the sounds of asphalt, wooden benches, and carpets, touch the handle and feel the moisture of his palm, and finally, to get to know him better, to slip out through the keyhold of the suitace and sit down on his shoulder.

Time goes from suitcase to suitcase; you step out of one suitcase and into another. The house where you live is a suitcase; you go to work – it's a suitcase; you enter a woman – she's a suitcase; you have a child – it's a suitcase. You are a suitcase too. When you die, you're put in a coffin, which is a suitcase…

Mendeleev was an expert when it came to making suitcases. He would meticulously choose the wood, the calf leather, silver-plated locks, and then labor for days in his workshop, perfecting his art.

Perhaps he was polishing his own memories and secrets, stuffing the suitcases with them and keeping them there…

There was an incident in my life which has not yet given me peace.

I was little. My father would say that dwarves lived in the suitcases who would wake up at night and run around the room, entering the mouths of people as they slept. That was why we should not poke around in suitcases, we would anger the mischievious dwarves. He would also say that the one of the dwarves looked like me – the same mole on his forehead, a large belly, and slightly moody. I really wanted to find them, especially my doppelganger, and did not listen to my father. I would poke around in all the suitcases for days, hoping to find those merry dwarves and become their friend. While playing in the yard, I talked about the dwarves to a friend of mine that had the color of water. He was always sad and withdrawn. When he heard what I had to say, he moved his melon-like long face and the lid above his left eye started to twitch.

"Your father has lied to you," he said in a low voice. "There are no dwarves in suitcases, that's where children go to lie down after they die, and they cry in fear at night." The boy fell quiet and put his index and middle fingers to rub the head of a one-legged sparrow he was holding. He had rescued the bird from between two electric wires.

"Children don't die. You're trying to fool me. Adults die," I said, depressed.

"Children die," the boy continued, "I know that children die so that they don't grow old," he put the sparrow in a pastry box and left.

After that, I searched all the suitcases for dead children and grew afraid of hearing them cry at night. I used a hammer to break the locks and open the suitcases, emptying them of the clothes, towels, handkerchiefs, belts, and ties they held. I then filled them with water, scratched them, cut them with scissors, pulled the lining off their walls, thinking that I would find children curled up somewhere. My mother had heard me… I told her that I had damaged all the suitcases we had at home, I said I was looking for dead children, I wanted to see them, they were crying at night and not letting me sleep. My mother sat down next to me and said in a soft voice:

"Nobody was crying in your room last night. You heard yourself crying. There are no dead children in our suitcases and, in general, children don't die, they simply leave. Go to sleep." My mother did not tell me where children went.

When I met that friend again, he was using a plastic spade to fill his stocking with sand.

"You tricked me, there are no dead children in suitcases, because children don't die," I said. He held out the spade and said,

"Pour some sand."

I took the spade and started filling the stocking with sand.

"I know, your mother must have lied to you," the boy continued. "Don't believe her. She's lying to you to keep you from being scared because, when you believe that children die, you will die too. There's a suitcase in our house which has a child living in it. I see him…"

My friend took the spade and, somehow dragging his sand-swollen legs, went away.

Years later, I found out that the boy had secretly removed his dead newborn brother from his little coffin and put him in a suitcase, so that they would not bury him.

THE BOX

The edges of the ivory box have melted because of the body heat. Komitas' face has been etched by a small needle on its yellowish cover, with the words "A memento from Alek to Manush, 1938" wiggling beneath it. It's a small box, almost Grandma's size…

I had seen the box two times – my Grandma would always keep it near her. She would put it under her pillow when she slept, she would stuff it between her breasts when she baked *lavash*, she would place it in her flowery underwear, my father would tell me. A funny thing had happened once. My petite Grandma had fallen awkwardly into the toilet bowl, somehow managed to climb out, and then noticed that the box was missing. She had caused havoc in the village. Finally, a group of burly men, drenched in sweat, ended up taking the toilet apart, shoveling out the shit, digging through it to find the box, and returning it to her.

My Grandma had showered blessings on all of them, sacrificed a pigeon on Sunday, cooked rice, and served them all that food.

At the end of her life, she was like a fruit that had fallen from a tree, the uniform wrinkles on her neck had softened and grown longer.

She was always crying – at funerals, on birthdays, on New Year's Day, when she met people, when she laughed, when she was angry, when she recalled something, always… she was like a never-ending pool of tears. This surprised me, I wanted to understand it better.

"Why are you crying, Grandma?"

She was crying again.

What was in the box? Perhaps it was a large diamond that she could not give up, or a document that had great importance…

My Grandma would warm water under the sun's rays everyday, which she would use to wash her feet. She was in a great mood that day, she threw her towel aside and used her apron to dry her feet. She kissed my forehead and said that she was going to die at three o'clock. She asked me to shave the beard growing on her chin and tie the shawl with the red roses on her head. And then she left, climbing into bed.

She died at three fifteen because her crying dragged on a bit longer than planned. It was a regular day at home, Grandma had lived a very long life.

We bathed her in the little boat that we had always used to wash our wool. I did as she asked – I shaved the beard and rubbed down her chin with a softening cucumber cream, then covered her head with the rose-covered shawl bought in Akhaltsikhe. When we folded her salty arms across her chest, something rolled out to the floor from her palm – it was the box. I picked it up and opened it. A clump of hair tied in twine lay silently on an embroidered handkerchief. It was the hair of her husband who had died in the war…

"Grandma, Grandma!" I had once happened to see her rubbing that hair on her cheekbones and in her wrinkles, feeling the weight, length, coarseness of each hair, then bringing it to her mouth and dampening it with her tongue… The only explanation that had come to my mind was that she was going senile at her advanced age…

"So, what did you do with the hair?" I asked my father.

"We used the same twine to tie the hair to the wood of the coffin, she took it with her. But you know what the strangest thing was?" Father continued, "My grandfather was twenty-two years old when he went to fight in the war, but when I opened the box, his hair had grown completely white."

JAZZ

They rush through one's veins. The walls are elastic. Large and small trumpets are partly in red stream water. Spinning round and round. Click-click, Da-ddy. They've been traveling for so many years, but they have forgotten everything in the world. Thirst. Hunger. Rest. The father and son trumpeter duo kept encouraging each other. The father would overtake his son, wave at him happily, and exclaim, "Giddy up, now! Faster, boy!" They were sweating. The father would disappear from view. The boy would strain his eyes and try to spot him. Where are you, Father? Which way did you turn? Did you slip into a capillary? Hello? Hello? Where are you? Toot, toot. The boy's trumpet touches a wall. He falls down. His hand slides into a hot orifice. There's only one tooth left in his father's mouth. Hey, Dad! Trumpet! There are no signs of consciousness. No pulse to be found. You're dead. You're a corpse. We're alone at home now. Everyone has left. Everyone. Who's everyone? You know… everyone. Everyone means all of them. Oh, everyone. I'm still here. I feel sorry. I'm still here, because I plan to do some killing. If you so desire. Are you writing, son? I'm writing. I'm writing to prove a point to you. To prove that I am nothing. Listening to jazz? Well. Raise the volume. Fill the glasses. What a fantastic trumpet! A real requiem. Is that your beloved Davis, or is it Dizzy? It doesn't matter. You've done a good job with the furniture in your room. Woven chair. Umbrella. Coffee table. Books. Miniature paintings. Jack Daniels. Literary magazines and journals. Jazz. Wonderful! Death can smell the bait. It's on the way. Raise the volume. Us, boy. Us. I had never heard a performance like that. The train coming from afar was whistling mournfully. It was a wonderful tune. The trumpet was rising like a horse taking to its hind legs. Calmly. Slowly. Like a madman. The pitch curdles the blood. It rises. Lowers. Runs. Stops. Waits. Pause. Leap. We're going to die, son. You and I. Gods don't die. Jesuses do. They die. Die. Gods die with the help of Jesuses, son. Raise the volume. Fulfil my last wish.

Two tunes in the middle of the room. Us. We're alone. I'm obliged to carry out my father's last wish. Are there any teeth left in your mouth? Bring the pliers. I pull his last tooth. I put a piece of cotton in the wound. There's a knock on the door. It's either that woman selling curds or your mother. It doesn't matter. Turn up the volume. Thousands of cats leap out of the trumpets. Cats the size of ants. They fill the room. The cats have no eyes. They walk over me and Father. They slam their heads against the walls. I know what we're going to do now, Father. I take out two sturdy pieces of rope from the cupboard. Mountain climbing rope. Where did these come from? Your mother bought them. Is she in the cupboard? Yes, she's sitting in a suitcase, listening to jazz. So she hasn't left us? She was holding the ropes. Turn up the volume so that we don't feel how they hurt our necks. I tie the ropes to the ceiling lamps. Bring them a bit closer. I sling one of the knots around Father's neck. The other is around mine. We push the stools away. Wonderful. Two hanging trumpets. Two meaty trumpets. Two pieces of nothing. Father and son. How do you feel, Father, hanging from the ceiling? Enjoying it? This is the best position for an intimate conversation. Let's massage our bodies a bit so that we get drunk sooner. That's good. Fill the glasses. Gulp, gulp, gulp, gulp, gulp, gulp. Good job, you've remembered to bring the bottle with you. Raise the volume. The blind cats are enchanted. They are frozen on the couches, chairs, listening to the music. Let's have a toast to you. Let's have nothing to you. Thank you. Do you remember me, son? I remember. How? I remember the first time you bought me a bike. I remember the first and last time you put a piece of candy in my pocket. I remember when you pulled my pants down and grabbed my willy, so that I could urinate. I remember when you beat me in front of my grandmother and grandfather, so that they would be satisfied. I remember when I got into university, you sacrificed a sheep for me. I remember when you took a beating with me at the hands of those whelps from the building next to ours, the ones that had been teasing me. I remember tasting the tomato omlet your mistress had made. I remember when we went to visit one of your patients together – they offered me some fruit juice and raisins. I remember that when the coffin had scared me, you let me embrace you. I remember that I had stuck to your narrow chest like the skin of an apple. I remember that I disturbed you and mother that night. I remember that I slapped you, and you cried like me. The rope is very tight. Someone's knocking on the door. Can you imagine the woman selling curds coming in now and seeing us? I remember a background of jazz with a father and son hanging from the ceiling. Fill the glasses, son. The parqueted floor is covered in timothy grass. The green, juicy grass goes up to our knees. Cats are replaced by curly-haired sheep with thick layers of fat between their legs. Baa, baa. They're grazing. Baa, baa. When you were a young boy, would you think about me, Father? I would think. But I didn't know that you would be born from my one thousandth ejaculation. I'm sorry. Really. As soon as you were born, I thought about the emptiness and regretted it. You are the soap bubble that I let go. I gave you life so that you may die. You are the one who will continue the game. You should think about your own child. Give him nothingness. I'll take him to trumpet lessons, so that he can play to forget about me. Remember, Father, the first time you poured petrol into your lungs? And then gas. Then shoe polish. Then whiskey. Cognac. Vodka. Rum. Wine. Mulberry, cornelian cherry vodka. Vinegar. My cologne. Remember? I remember. I would think – how come you aren't dying? I was shocked. Gods are slow to die. They torture everyone as they do so. I want to go numb. It's not working. To go numb and die. Without blood. Are you tired of ropes? Of this world. Of me. Of surgery. Of the woman selling curds. Of everyday work. Of the streets of Yerevan. Saryan Street. Tumanyan. Teryan. Marx. Coffin Street. Komitas. Baghramyan. Endless streets. The same endless memories. Aren't you tired? Fill the glasses. This is some wonderful jazz. Father, your legs are growing shorter. You're starting to look like that dwarf Kolol. Your head is the size of a tangerine. I'm dematerializing, son. By shrinking. Disappearing. Fearing. But I have to ask you something. A last request. What is it? Empty that syringe of morphine into my veins. Please. Where is this morphine from? I have a cancer patient, it's his painkiller. He'll die today. Screaming in pain. Because I've stolen his dose of medication. For myself. I want to self-destruct with your help. Your help. Aren't you tired? Hanging from the ceiling. Let's go down. Let's. They cut the ropes. They come down. They sit on the trumpets. They continue their journey. With jazz. Two trumpets. Father and son. A journey of decision. A journey of farewell. The hospital lights are brighter than the stars. Do you hear that patient screaming? His voice carries all the way here. I feel sorry for him, Father. Why did you steal his painkiller? It's all right, he's no longer with us. But I am unable to die. You have to help me. The dose of morphine is a large

one this time. You want me to kill you? With jazz? I want you to help me.
Fill the glasses. Remember, Father, how happy we were? When? When you
came home sober one day. That only happened once, son? Once. You see?
We were happy on one occasion in our lives. Let's drink to that one occasion.
Turn up the volume. It seems to be bringing my feelings back. Jazz was
created by slaves. Slaves. Who were not afraid of emptiness. Of destruction.
Not afraid. You will do a lot of crying when I am no longer with you. I'll
remember that. Turn up the volume, it is simply divine. They light a fire.
They lean the trumpets against the only tree in the room. His father uses a
surgical scalpel to disconnect his legs. He runs skewers through them. I'll
barbecue them nice and well soon, son. You'll taste your own father's legs.
Fill the glasses. The cognac is old. Sticky. Remember, Father, when you came
back from the war, and I didn't recognize you? Your dirty beard disgusted
me. Your human and inhuman stories. I recognized you later, remember,
when you were drunk and your hair stood on end, and when you seated me
on your knee? Remember? I recognized you from the curve of your knee.
Why did that happen? Why did I kill you? I didn't want to, honest. The
barbecue is ready. Open your mouth. I don't want to. As you wish. Father
uses a scalpel to remove his head. He puts a tomato in its place. We laugh.
You never lose your sense of humor. The patient's screaming grows more
and more deafening. Father barely manages to hold his body. His sole focus
is on the tomato. He's gripping the trumpet tightly with one hand, and the
other is holding on to the tomato that has replaced his head. A wonderful
scene. Fill the glasses. Women don't understand poets, son. Are you a poet,
Father? I'm not a poet but I drink like one. Does it hurt anywhere? It doesn't
hurt. Do you see me now? I feel you. You feel me? Does that hurt? Very
much, my son. But it's not a physical pain in any sense. When you feel it,
your bowels go loose. You always want to go. You feel nauseated. You stand
near the window. You're scared. You call your wife and say something inco-
herent. You come and go to the bathroom a hundred times at night in vain.
You open the refrigerator door and close it. Why are you using your hand
to hold that tomato? Well, there has to be something in my head's place,
right? You're right. Can you imagine? You're going to wake up. And I am no
more in your world. My constant calls are no more. My hateful face is no
more. No shame. No whiskey, cognac, no miraculous discovery by Sertürner.
No nighttime screaming. No beating. My smell is no more. My clothes are

no more. Slippers. Underwear. My plate is no more. The depression from where I was sitting. I am no more. Turn up the volume. Let's drink one last time while listening to jazz to the path we have traversed. It's powerful. Two trumpets in the middle of the room. The window is open. There is nothing below. Father jumps out the window. His right hand remains in the room. Fill the glasses. The tempo is crazy. The musicians are geniuses. This is an exceptional performance. Passion. Fire. Sizzling. White-yellowish tinged needle-like crystals. The hand smiles. Remember my right hand? I remember. I remember when you slapped me with that right hand. I remember when you taught me how to shave for the first time with that right hand. I remember when you cleaned my snotty nose with that right hand. I remember when you woke me up with that right hand so that I would not be late to school. I remember when you would inject something into your left arm with that right hand. I remember when you would rub mother's right shoulder with that right hand. I remember. Dogs were eating Father's body down below. The hand caresses my thin hair. Don't worry, I no longer feel any pain. Never mind the dogs. Let them get a piece of me. Surgeon's meat tastes good. Fill the glasses. Good boy. The hand throws itself across my shoulder. That soft, delicate hand. Someone's knocking on the door. It's the woman selling curds. Can you imagine? What if she comes in and sees us? The boy sitting on the couch, his father's hand on his neck. Listening to jazz. Turn up the volume. The syringe is in the drawer. Take it out. Jazz is unique music. Tie a tourniquet. Now, fulfil my request. Good boy. I'm going numb. Slowly. Slowly. Piece by piece. Good job, my son. My family. Empty that whole syringe. Don't be scared. Push me away from yourself. Destroy me. The arm shudders. Grabs my wrist. Its veins submerge like fish. He goes blue. Foams. Glazes over. Stops breathing. The boy and the arm. In the middle of the room. Turn up the volume. Jazz. Jazz. How would fathers and sons live without you? Father? Is that it? Are you gone? You still have something left to drink. At least empty the glass on the windowsill. Are you leaving me alone? Alone. Poor Father. Poor glass.

WORK, WORK

I love you tomorrow… My mobile phone dances to James Brown's wailing. Something buzzes inside me. The sweat-drenched bedsheet cuts through my dream and reality. I bury my head in the down pillow. I love you today. It continues. Jesus, I love you… My head… my head… boom… it has exploded. I wake up in the city of Yerevan – Arabkir 21st Street, apartment 24, it is thirteen o'clock, or one in the afternoon. It is never too late to start the day. Thank the Lord I am not alone. In Venezuela, Luisa is rubbing her eyes, Foé is running to the bathroom to pee, Murad is still asleep in Albania. We serve in a united army – the regiment of the unemployed.

I sit up in bed. Sweet sleepiness is still holding me in its embrace, like an orgasm. My fingers somehow manage to feel and find the table stuck to my bed. That last Esse is like an oasis in an excruciating desert. Swaying like a sailor, I step out onto the balcony and, blinded by the brightness, I light the cigarette. The smoke slowly caresses my lungs. Wham… crash… grrr… a cloud of dust… "Buildings? Huh? It's quite incomprehensible. On the one hand, we have hunger and poverty, while on the other, we see Northern Avenue and huge, misshapen cars." In reality, this ruin and chaos is an inseparable part of my soul. There is not enough oxygen – the warm brings a blended flavor of petrol and gas to my mouth. I hear sounds of laughter. On the posh balcony opposite mine, lush with all kinds of decorative plants, the neighbor's teenage daughters are peeking out towards me. The flowery pattern on my underwear is causing them amusement, making me look stupid. The mewing that my cat has started is the signal of a job that needs to be carried out. "Yes, Chocolate, I'll feed you in a minute." I walk through the narrow footpath between scattered books, magazines, unwashed plates, stacks of records, and empty beer bottles, making it to the handle of the fridge door. The bag of milk is sitting alone, with no companions, on the aluminum rack; it turns its frightened gaze to my hungrily shimmering eyes. I piously split the milk into two portions. I pour Chocolate's share into a clay bowl decorated with fish pictures, while my portion whitens an aluminum pot placed on the lit gas stovetop. I don't know how other unemployed people start their day, how they freshen up their heavy and buzzing heads – coffee, mate, green or black tea. I am in the category of unemployed people that start the day with cocoa. It's an issue of taste and preference, I guess… Only after that refreshing drink has been consumed does the "What should I do?" begin, which places me in front of a huge, concrete obstacle. My television had conclusively burned out a few days ago. I had raped it. It had been chattering away day and night, without the time to take a breath. I would sink into a hysteric state of depression when there was a power cut, interrupting the emanating magical rays. The milk bubbled. I prepare my favorite cocoa and pour it into the only surviving cup, then walk around in the room. I had not slept for three nights, I was reading *Hospital* by Khanjyan. After closing the book, I began to listen to the happy love games the flies played – by the way, flies are great teachers when you have a spare moment. Enchanted by those games, I was transforming in my mind, joining in their carefree fun. I was thinking about the unique lives that flies lead – they have no job, no homeland; the whole planet was their natural habitat.

I fell asleep at dawn. I had a dream. I was walking in the streets of Yerevan – sad, worried, rejected. As I walked through the crowd, my body got goosebumps – people were walking without their heads but, for some reason, I could feel the weight of them staring at me and I was enveloped in a fog of embarrassment. I hastened my steps. I notice a huge oval mirror in a street corner and quickly hand over my external appearance to the judgment of that piece of glass. I was rooted to my spot in shock. In my place, I could see a completely naked body, covered by flowing drops of sweat. I did not understand what I was supposed to do next. The curious, headless crowd surrounded me. A policeman appeared from somewhere. Excited, he began to describe the rules of behavior in public spaces. I laughed in shock, unable to understand the seriousness of the situation. The policeman's surprise kept blending with my meaningless mirth, interrupted by one-minute intervals. The policeman's head then turned into that of an old goat with sharp horns, a dense beard – one that had just been milked and, enjoying that sensation of lightness, was bleating with soul-enchanting consistency. In the end, all of us went through the infinity of the mirror…

It's my mobile phone.

I'm tired.

I switch off my phone. Chocolate suppresses his nausea as he finishes his milk. When it comes to eating, our pathetic menu has not changed in the past month – milk and bread. Given a choice between action and inaction, I find inaction much closer to my heart. It's wonderful when you don't act, when you simply try to live, but very soon you start to receive messages from your body that slowly turn into threats. I very often revolt against action through my inaction, and I like that wave of rebellion, even though I am really tired by that farce of life that everyone plays out, without exception. Whether I like it or not, I have also taken up a role in this supposed reality. I have learned to live for tomorrow, when everything will turn out well, when there will be good times and opportunities; such optimism shoud be cause for wonder, but death has a way of putting everything in its place, managing every dream and thought. I know that death is the only paradise that awaits me… Whatever. I empty my cup of cocoa with a final sip, quickly put on some clothes and leave the house.

When I press the half-burned button in the elevator, I make the sign of the cross. I pray for it not to stop on the fifth floor, but when we truly want something, God's will is always the opposite. The doors of the elevator open right on the fifth floor. The smell of bad quality tobacco irritates my nostrils. My neighbor, Suren, is a sixty-year-old army veteran-turned-tailor, filled with a love for life. His monkeyish physique causes a kind of awkwardness. His swollen, tomato-like red face and that uneven nose rich in fleshy meatballs are reminiscent of a jolly character from some kind of cartoon. His lower lip hangs, blended with bits of his nose and tobacco. When he speaks, his blue eyes pop out like someone with a thyroid condition, and his long, furry orangutan arms seem like memories of an incomplete process of evolution…

"Oh, you useless creature, is that you? How are you?"

He walks into the elevator like a clubfooted bear.

"I'm good, Uncle Suren, how are you?"

"I'm doing very well, going to see my lover, hee hee!"

He is really getting on my nerves.

"Did you get a job?" he focuses on the question in his mind. If we meet on a thousand and sixty occasions, he will ask this question a thousand and sixty times…

"I left my old job and I got a new one a couple of days ago. I'm going to work now," I reply, depressed.

This upsets him and he spews particles of spit and tobacco to the left and right.

"You lying rascal! You haven't found a job, you're making it up. You know how many people like you have been run through by my sword? Hee, hee, hee." He continues, his head swinging, "I've found an old lady near the market. Man, am I giving it to her! Am I giving it to her! Hee, hee, hee…"

Oh God, I understand that you don't want to open the gates of heaven, but please allow the doors of this elevator to do so, I can't take it anymore! And, it's a miracle – my prayers are heard, the doors open. I leap out, my forehead covered in cold sweat.

These run-ins with my neighbor turn into absurd scenes. I've even tried leaving my apartment at different times in the day to test the probability of this ridiculous event and, to my surprise and misery, I have been unable to avoid a face-to-face meeting; it's as if he was informed of my every move… Oh, you useless creature, is that you? When I hear that voice, the blood clots in my veins, it's like someone pours muddy water into my soul, burning any new saplings that may have just sprouted buds. A miserable reality, the figure of God, the pointless determination to tempt or be tempted, I don't know what it is; in this situation of disagreement and confusion, the thought of suicide invades my mind and starts to plant roots there. "Suicide is an escape, I will trick life, laugh like Homer as I bring it to its knees, I will revolt against the pointlessness of existence, although the expectation of something new, which is hidden deep in my soul, will keep shamelessly preserving a kernel of hope in my departing consciousness to the very end."

I walk along pothole-ridden Komitas Street to Barekamutyun metro station. They tore this street up a year ago and laid it to ruin, offering hope through lavish promises that they would complete the renovation work on time and I would be able to walk day and night on my favorite pavements. But I guess they were lying yet again. Yes, they were lying…

I go into the underground crossing of the metro station. The subterranean air throbs in my airways. The beggar I see all the time has frozen in the same pose. His coat hardened with the same dirt, his ragged army pants, his Yeghvard sneakers, a big toe sticking out of the hole in the leather… The most amusing thing is his natural hairstyle – unwashed since time immemorial, hard as wood, singed here and there. He looks like a typical rock star, or a clown that had been banished from the circus ten years ago. His facial features are delicate – a broad forehead, a sharp aquiline nose, a hard and slightly protruding chin, but the misery in his eyes devastates me from inside at that very moment, depriving my quest of any meaning, sounding to me like a harbinger of death from Gabriel's horn. In the next moment, the beauty of suffering takes over me, and I am unable to move my gaze away from the distance in his eyes. I am terrified and amazed by the complete absence of concern, by his inert calm, which is more characteristic of prophets. It feels like he has achieved nirvana, he has received responses to questions without answers, he quietly derides the hollow concerns of passers-by, the way they run around, not knowing where they are going and why. I was convinced that the beggar had discovered the center – he had found solace, learned to adapt to life's absurdities, leaning his shoulder against a point from which it would be difficult for the ground to give away under him. Lying in bed, I would sometimes be worried – did he really need the spare change I left him, or the single cigarette or piece of bread, or even the shot of vodka that could all serve as a miniscule occasion of happiness for him? Using the inductive method, I think that the beggar is much closer to the center than I am, and this disappoints me a little… And, eventually, dear reader, if you truly continue to exist, I should say that the beggar really doesn't care for any of this. He will never think that it is possible for a boy to ponder all night about how he lives his life – no, this process is endlessly repeating like it's on a loop. Boy. Beggar. People. Spare change.

Let's get back to the story. I feel around in my pocket with my fingers, take out the change, but then regret it. I have lots of expenses, I'm making things difficult for myself again. I talk to myself and ask him for forgiveness, then quickly walk away. I had got a job in one of the internet clubs on Abovyan Street as a coordinator. I say hello to my coworkers and sit down in front of a computer. A girl steps out of my boss's office a little while later and turns to me…

"Step into the room for a minute, yeah?"

I am a bit flustered as I get up from the computer and quickly tidy my unruly hair in front of the mirror before going to the boss's office.

"Artak, how are you, man?" the thirty-something smartly dressed young man says, slurping his coffee.

"I'm fine, thanks…"

"It's true that you've been working here a very brief time, but I'm satisfied so far," the boss continued, enjoying a Mozart chocolate with his coffee – my stomach shrivels. "He'll probably offer me one," the thought crosses my mind.

"There's this delicate situation. I'm happy with your work, but I'm firing you today…"

My heart starts to beat insanely fast.

"Is there a reason?" I mutter dully.

"Well, my friend, a family member has asked me to arrange a job for his nephew. I can't turn him down, he's as close as a brother, so I've given him your job…" slu-u-u-urp, it's like he's swallowing me.

"Okay, whatever you say. Goodbye…"

I open the door, he calls out after me.

"Hey wait, hang on, man!" He takes out a crumpled five-thousand dram note from his wallet. "Take the money you've earned so far before you leave."

I take the money and leave. In the bathroom, I laugh as I cry, but the time for producing tears seems to be in the past. I need to find a new job, visit some offices, throw myself out there, subject myself to indignity, try again and again, throwing myself out there once more. What can I do? I need work, work….

Numbed with joy, I walk through the crowd. I don't know why, losing my job had filled me with pure joy. When I left my family, they had laughed. They said that I would soon appear at their doorstep, whining like a hungry dog. But I had survived so far – not bad, eh? I have no problem giving up our national mindset and I had now become indifferent to that insecurity of being cruel to people – you don't have a job? Then you're not a human being. You're a tramp or a loafer. They don't care that there are no jobs around. I had ended up in a scandalous situation last year. I was working as a waiter in a café called Smile. One evening, I had been told to take over an order of cocktails from table 9 – a pink flamingo and a fiesta. I walked up to the table with a tray. They were my neighbors, a married couple. The wife was a senior teacher at a school, the husband had opened his own dentistry practice.

"Artak? Hey! What are you doing here," the smell of her fluff struck against my face.

"I work here," I replied calmly, placing the cocktails on their table.

"What work do you do?" the dentist asked, flicking out a piece of shawarma from between his teeth.

"I'm a waiter."

"Really? Wow, man, I didn't expect that from you!"

His wife threw me an acid look and jumped into the conversation.

"Do your mother and father know what you're up to?"

"I'm not doing anything wrong. I'm working."

"You're not a poof, are you? There are some normal jobs out there, and you're here serving people coffee and stuff?" The tipsy dentist was shouting.

"Please talk softly, everyone's looking at us."

"Oh, so you're feeling embarrassed now, you little whelp? Is that what you are?"

I could no longer bear it. I put the tray aside and spat out whatever came to my mind at him. In a few minutes, I established that there was nothing shameful in being a waiter, what was more embarrassing was that people like him and his wife still existed in society. The whole café sat in stony silence, taking in my vehement vocabulary. The manager fired me on the spot.

I blend into the gray carefreeness of the city. Chocolate will be happy with the food I bring home today, that will soften his contempt for me. I step into the bookstore Bookinist and buy a collection of Tanizaki's stories – an illustrated paperback. I step outside and walk in the direction of Saryan Street. I can enjoy a cigar today too, blow out the smoke of temporary happiness, surround myself in a thin membrane, create an unreal reality outside of reality.

I've always had a thing for the shop Don Cigar. The salesperson there is a wonderful young woman. We have a long chat about this and that, she never asks me about my job. I pay for a Jose El Piedra. I can also afford to dream about that magical world of cafés now.

As I walk, my emotions run ahead of me. Once in a while, my loud laughter is replaced by the tears streaming down my cheeks, then by some chuckling, followed a short while later by inconsolable sorrow. After that, I start to skip and sing my favorite song. A café is always ready to welcome a

customer with open arms. I sit down, order a cup of coffee and light my cigar with slow satisfaction, then start to flip through the pages of my book…

Life seems to be unnaturally pleasant but, suddenly, my whole body is
covered in goosebumps and a familiar voice rings out from so close that
not believing it would be self-deceit.

"Oh, you useless creature, is that you? How are you?"

THE CHRISTMAS TREE

He opened the box with his eyes closed, his breath held. The colorful ornaments were quietly asleep on the cream-colored paper. On the surface of those decorations, he saw the sad reflection of his face and the curvy shadows of his pointy hair. In the box, there were layers upon layers of ornaments and streamers which adorned their Christmas tree every year. The small, plastic Christmas tree that his parents had bought in the city of Vanadzor a long time ago, even before he was born. Its skeleton had grown weak over the years, its green leaves had melted here and there from the heat of the lights. Every year, when he placed the tree, his father would use a copper wire to fasten the tree's thin trunk to the four-legged base, so that it would not fall over.

At first, the Christmas tree looked like a winter sparrow – withdrawn and miserable. But once they had placed it in the living room and finished decorating it, everything changed. As he lay in bed, he would watch as the tree would suddenly light up, and his heart would start to beat quickly. He would hear someone's bells ringing in the distance, snow crunching underfoot, and mischievous voices whispering. He was most upset when he saw pieces of broken ornaments in the box. Lying in cotton, those shards would emit rainbow-colored rays of reflected light. He would open his mouth and try to swallow the sparkling rays, but they would always bend in the pepper shaker and disappear.

* * *

December 31[4] was the only day when he would take the ornaments out of the box and give them to his father, who would then carefully hang then from one of the branches of the tree. It was the only day when, during this exercise, his fingers would happen to touch his father's and cause his whole body to shiver. That touch, so unplanned but much awaited in the depths of his soul, caused the boy a kind of mild but profound pain. December 31 was the only day that he impatiently awaited… But his father did not return this time. He watched his mother's irregular pacing from a crack in the door. Her tears were drip-dropping on her floury apron, mixing with it and growing thicker as they slid down, before coming to a stop. His mother's tears were like snowballs. She was packing his father's suitcase. Piling up his pants and shirts, then pouring them out, and starting to pack them again, fighting against her own actions. She calmed down a little after a while, sat down on the edge of the bed, and lit a cigarette with trembling hands. She leaned her chin on her hands, slipped her pinky into the space between her lips, and closed her eyes. His mother would smoke only when she felt helpless, and her beauty would double at moments like that one.

A stranger walked in, picked up his father's suitcase, and said that the situation on the war front was terrible, they were unable to cope with the number of wounded, the people needed a surgeon – they were waiting for him. The suitcase was like his father's final piece of presence in the house. When that man took the suitcase and closed the door after he left, the house was enveloped in an uncertain, heavy emptiness.

* * *

Perhaps there, in the hospital, there would also be a Christmas tree, and when his father walked past it, he would stop for a minute and remember that their own Christmas tree at home was impatiently waiting to be decorated. Lying there in bed, he thought about all the children that had been wounded by shelling and bullets, the ones that lay dying, staring with longing at the lights on the hospital Christmas tree. Perhaps the children would forget that they were wounded when they saw the Christmas tree, perhaps

....

[4]   The Armenian Apostolic Church celebrates Christmas on January 6, the Christmas tree is a symbol associated with the New Year, not Christmas.

they would forget that they no longer had legs, or arms, because the lights on a Christmas tree are magical, they make you forget your pain. Then he would constantly remember the story that his father's friend, who was also fighting on the frontlines in the war, had told with laughter the previous year – how one of the guys in his regiment had been a sharpshooter, firing perfect shots to kill two kids on the enemy's side that had not been careful enough when coming near their trenches and trying to cut off a tree for the holidays. That man laughed two times – once before he told the story and once when he had finished it. That final laugh had the sound of gunfire splitting the air.

* * *

He put on his coat and left the house. It was snowing. He stopped under a streetlamp and raised his face upward. The snowflakes slowly moved through the bluish light and landed on his face, settling on the edges of his lips, his cheeks. He liked the weightless softness of the snowflakes lodging on his face and that almost untouchable moment stroking his skin. "I'm a Christmas tree for these snowflakes," the boy thought.

He walked along the length of the five-floor building. Whenever the lights of a Christmas tree flickered from inside any of the first-floor windows, he would stop and try to look inside. The people living in these unfamiliar apartments felt so dear to him that he could hardly resist the unbearable desire to knock on the door and go inside… to enter and simply stand silently in front of the Christmas tree, allowing the flickering lights to ripple along his face. He would have wanted to see how they went about decorating their trees, the boxes from which their ornaments and streamers emerged, but all the trees on the other side of the windows had already been decorated and lit.

* * *

He went upstairs to his apartment. There was a crowd in front of his door. It was ajar. He could hear his mother crying. There were family members and strangers inside. The men were smoking, the women sitting in chairs were rocking back and forth. His paternal uncle walked up to him, hugged his shoulders, and kissed him. "We just got a call, they said that the hospital was shelled, completely destroyed…" He understood. His father was gone. He was gone because he was not at home. Just to be sure, the boy went into each of the rooms of the apartment – he looked in the kitchen, on the balcony, among the crowd that had gathered. He could not find him. He went and sat down in the couch in the dark living room.

The bells sounded, ringing in the New Year. The boy closed his eyes and opened them a short while later. In the corner of the living room, near the Christmas tree, stood his father, wearing a white doctor's coat. He was pressing his fingers to his lips and winking, a soft smile on his face. The boy slowly walked up, then sat down silently next to the box, took out an ornament and gave it to his father. His father picked it up, carefully hung it on a branch of the tree and then held out his hand, caressing his pointy hair. His fingers seemed to stay in his hair for an eternity…

The lights of the Christmas tree burned brightly.

Deep in his soul, he felt the miracle arrive.

WHEN REMEMBER YOU ALWAYS

It's not easy being a neighborhood and seeing that wooden box ceremoniously turned around three times. It's not lying in that box, unable to see that street you know so well, with its three intersections, and the writing on the cobbler's booth that says: "Cold watermelons". It does not matter whether it is a cat in the box or a human being – they are both equally important for the street and deserve the same love, they shape the neighborhood into what it is. It's not easy standing alone and in silence before the membrane that separates dreams from sleep, and to feel the soul of a weeping boy there, whose grandmother and grandfather are trying to console him, they will give him lollipops and candy, they will explain that the clown is playacting, nobody has really beaten him up. He will start a second wave of tears. The children will turn and curiously examine the face burning with tears. In the meantime, he will steal half a glance through the gaps in his fingers and look at the clown, who will hear a voice below him that differs from laughter and will suddenly smile broadly and hop around, playing a few tricks and thinking that he would be able to change the boy's mood that way. But, seeing that nothing is changing, he will sit down on his stool and, depressed, will hang his head. And the boy's crying will come close to ruining the show, it will cause real concern for the rest of the patient audience. His grandmother and grandfather will be forced to quickly put on his coat and urge him out of the circus, and his sobbing will gradually be forgotten only in the lights visible through the window of the streetcar. Later, when he sees a tangerine for the first time, he will think that it's a yellow ball, he will pick it up from the box and start to play. The peel will tear, and a sourly sweet juice will pour on his palm. He will peel the tangerine completely, put it on the cover of the box and look at it with mystified eyes for a long time, and will then pick it up and start to eat it, bursting the meaty pieces of its flesh beneath the roof of his mouth. At university, he will not go down to the underground crossing of the Yeritasardakan metro station with his friends between classes to eat a shawarma. He will buy a kilogram of tangerines from the old man across the street and, finding a suitable spot to sit near the Konica store, he will start to juggle them, throwing the round fruits into the air one by one. Passers-by will have different reactions. The guys will laugh, light another cigarette, the men will pretend they haven't seen him, women weighed under by their many bags will cast a fleeting glance before quickening their goosy pace. Only the children and the crazies will be enchanted, watching as the yellow traces of the balls will go up into the sky, come down, spin in the air, merge with the sparrows and the seeds of plane trees. Mothers will pull their children by the hand with a reprimand, but even as they leave, they will not turn their eyes away from the tangerines, until it is completely out of their field of vision…

Death throes are not painful, they are simply a repetition of your child-hood dreams. You are lying in a boat, leaning on soft pillows. There are Christmas tree ornaments hanging from the sky on thin threads, touching your head. The boatman is standing at the end, wearing a flame-colored cape, a wide-brimmed broadcloth hat on his head. He bows respectfully and smiles at you. At first, you do not recognize the clown you had seen at the circus years ago. You want to get up from your place and say hello, but your body is pleasantly numb, you are filled with a kind of uncertain absence, you are mute, like your tongue is not in your mouth. You automatically take your hand to your left cheek – only emptiness there, you bring your hand down in the same direction, but there is nothing. When you look with your right eye, you notice that the left half of your body is missing. The boatman senses the panic of anxiety and depression taking over your soul. "Try to come to me," a mild voice can be heard through the mist. You make a major effort and somehow manage to get up from your place, and you grab hold of the ornaments in order to move toward the boatman. "Don't worry about it, the right side of my body is missing too. We have to merge together and then we can continue to row the boat." Your body easily fuses with the boatman's in the white water's reflection. You continue to row the boat together. As soon as you reach the shore, you separate. "I'll go my own way from here, take care…" I will recall this dream for the last time when my friend's little boy,

　　　　　　　　　　　　　　　　　　　　　

Areg, will pick up a tangerine from the table and pass it on to me. When I meet the child for the first time, I will be filled with a strange sensation. He will also understand at once and hug my neck tightly. I will be too embarrassed to tell his parents that the boy is the boatman from my dream, the one with the flame-colored cape – they would never believe me anyway. The boy will be unable to speak, he will take a few steps back, stand in front of me and, when his eyes come closer, I will see the shimmering Christmas tree ornaments and a floating boat in his pupils... The skeletons of newly constructed buildings will devour the functional part of the street, leaving only a few small ramshackle huts stuck to each other at the shoulders. He will stop in front of the narrow, stone-walled, arched alley separating the huts from each other. He will have to stoop quite a bit to enter the alleyway and will walk around six meters like that, until he gets to the start of the courtyard. "It looks like it's meant for dogs, although it's tough to imagine a huge wolfhound fitting in there..." Who are you looking for, son? The voice will be heard from beneath the asphalt... He will turn around and see no one... Who are you looking for son? Come closer... He will stoop and stick his head in, he will look into the darkness... I'm underneath your shoe... The voice will be heard again... He will stare at the ground... If she does not speak and you don't hear her voice, you would never guess that she's just another old lady. You'd think she's a native African statue, or a mangy, hairless rat... It's difficult to make out from up here whether she is sitting or standing, her long, sharp chin touches the ground, her headscarf gives off a musty smell and the location of her mouth is betrayed by the lit cigarette... Careful, son, don't step on me, it will bring you bad luck... Do you want a nut? And it's true, one more step and your shoe's thick insole will squish the old woman... Your foot is left hanging in the air... Have you come to take us out, son? Hee, hee... Do you want sunflower seeds, peanuts, roasted pumpkin seeds, raw fruits, almonds? Hmmm... "No, I'm looking for the dentist that lives on this street, he used to be a clown," you will say to yourself... Bah! Why do you need that idiot? Ah, you must be a mime... She will continue with a wily intonation... "I..." How many laughs can you remember in life, hmm? You must be an idiot too, like your dentist. You want to clown around and make us laugh – what good does laughing do if my stomach is empty? Hee, hee, cough... Do you want some peanuts? "Listen, grandma, your stomach may be empty, but you're still laughing..." Me? Look at this guy, will you? Did you hear anyone laugh here? Get lost, you street mongrel… The old woman will grow angry, her chin quivering, saliva dripping out of her mouth… Don't make me get up or I'll smash your face in… "Sisi, Sisi, oh how I long to hug you… That sack of sunflower seeds you always have, the one in which you live and sleep, that cracked vodka shotglass with a piece of rubber at the bottom, your constant stream of cursing from dawn to dusk, and the saddest day of your life when your son came home from the war in a coffin. You couldn't believe it, Sisi. You timidly walked up to him unnoticed, scattering sunflower seeds and peanuts on his face, and then the whole street heard your voice with respect and sorrow…" Get up, don't pretend to be asleep… I've roasted some peanuts for you… Don't you want your mother's roasted peanuts? You don't want them? After your son's funeral, you lay down and, before going to bed, you announced to everyone that you were going to die. But did anybody hear you? The kids came over to see you every day, they took care of you, brought you hot meals, watered your cacti, combed your white hair, showed you pictures of your son… "Death did not accept you, Sisi. Death had no use for your old, rotten life. Only the street has a use for that; that is where your sack should forever be, full to the brim with your sectrets…." And one day… one cool and clear day, you got up and said, "Fuck you all, what is this nightrobe you've put on me?" And then you took out your sack from under your bed and put your roasting pan on the gas stove…

You will smile as you walk through Sisi, and you curl up as you advance. Her sweet curses will land against your back for a long time to come… The small space before the courtyard does not particularly impress you in any way… There are wooden doors in front of the huts on your left and right, short staircases, slippers of different sizes and quality piled up on top of each other at the entrances, and the same clotheslines cobwebbed everywhere. Her unnatural red hair will be visible from the cracks in the doors. "Who's going to paint your hair now?" Her freckled, broad face, the puffy two-sizes-too-large jacket that she's wearing, her long and bony fingers… "Hello…" you'll say. She won't respond, she'll pretend she didn't hear you. "Excuse me, could you please let me know where the dentist lives?" She will raise her head for a moment, and you will see her stony face in her blue eyes. "Her blue pupils are full of black grains of sand, sand from the sea, and there are green lines in the grains of sand, dark green lines, wavy leaves in the lines, branching veins in the leaves, with profound sorrow flowing through them… You have hardened like stone in your pupils and you cannot caress the dimples…" "How are you going to do this alone?" "I want to talk to you…" "If you can talk to the dead, I'll tell you where the grave is, and you can go talk." But she will start to cry suddenly, her eyelids pressing together like a spring. "You're torturing me… what do you want?" "I'm sorry…Fine… What can I say? Goodbye." Hopeless, you will leave, and then she'll shout… "Where are you going? Stop! Don't go. What have you done?" That familiar screaming will wake you up… You will step down from the wooden box placed in the middle of the room and follow her silently, you go to the kitchen. Wiping her tears, she will start to make coffee, she'll take out the Czech fruit plate you had given her from the drawer, and place it on the table… "You were completely naïve, nobody understood you, nobody understands the naïve and insane." "Insane? That reminds me. That reminds me of that crazy guy on our street named When, who had one of everything in life – one tooth, one father, one bottle of water, one pair of trousers, one shirt, one clown among his acquaintances, one dog, one dream. During the years of the war, he was the most useless beggar on the street because he was unable to do anything but twist his face this way and that. When was a toy in the hands of children. They would take off all his clothes, get on his back and run after him, whipping his ass with a birch. They would urinate in a bucket and pour it on his large head, burn off the abundant hair on his arms, fill his mouth with a mixture of apricot jam and sheep wool. But When would go crazier with happiness, hug the children, kiss their cheeks, arms, legs, and make new faces at them. Once, the children asked When to go up the tallest mulberry tree on the street and jump down from there. When had barely managed to stay alive. He had fallen among some rocks, broken his legs and shoulder, but kept smiling at the kids who were staring in horror at the small bones sticking out of his open wounds. After his old father died, his relatives handed When to a mental asylum. I remember the unforgettable timbre of his voice – the whole neighborhood had stepped out onto the street because of it. When was not giving in, he was knocking down all the orderlies with unimaginable strength and urging his small dog to attack, calling on me to help. Seeing that nothing was working, one of the doctors managed to slip an injection through that numbed him. Several of them worked together to put on a straitjacket. As they were stuffing him into the ambulance, I saw the whole history of the neighborhood stamped onto When's sad face. In his sleep, When could sense the farewell being given by the whole neighborhood…" "I can't believe that was the last cup coffee we had together…" "Well? Who's going to start your day for you next time?" My wife will talk to herself in a trembling voice as she holds the coffee kettle with a firm hand… "How I miss my classmates from college, that donut shop… You had fallen in love, it was sooo good… What wonderful years those were… You remained a child forever, and you made these children happy, they loved you so much… you would philosophize… you would say… laughter is the conscience of sorrow… and other things like that…" She will pour the coffee into the cups and put it on the table, with a tangerine next to your plate… "At least have some fruit…" You watch her fingers contract weakly, the way she holds her cup, her reserved and pretty sips, you will rest your head on her shoulder, look at the coffee you haven't touched… "You had found a job as a clown… You were so happy you were short of breath… Your parents hurt you, 'He's spineless,' they said with concern… Our family members and friends felt ashamed in your stead, only the kids of the neighborhood were crazy with joy. They gathered around you every day and you performed the pieces you had made up, and our neighborhood burst with laughter through the darkness; that laughter gave life to our streets…" He would cover his face with his hands… "You can go now… I guess you really wanted to leave…" You will take her cold hands, kiss her with your hot lips, and leave…

The cemetery, as always, was pleasantly silent. The air is saturated with the smell of flowers and incense, only the soft rustling of the wavy shadows. He walked on the soft path to the grassy hill, behind which a silvery spruce was growing. Walking around the hill along a red pebbled path, he entered the fenced graveyard and froze in place… The whole surface of the gravestone was covered in multicolor shiny stickers, amusing toys, there were balloons all around, numerous cards were glued to its surface. His heart beat rapidly as he removed one of them and read the text inside… then another… "The one the kids most…" he could not continue, he folded the card and put it in his pocket, but then felt bad, took it out again and placed it on the gravestone. His eyes fell upon the text in white paint beneath the name on the stone…

When remember you always… he lowered his hand slowly, holding his breath, and touched the words, ran his fingers along them for a long time… He stood up and walked towards the spruce. A small cricket cut across him and began to flap its green wings, drenched in the rays of the setting sun. He looked at the cricket's back and saw every moment of its departure.

SAD BOATS

He has a bun in his pocket, did you see it?

A bun. A bun, a raisin bun, yummy, yummy, thin, orange, crusty. You are standing near the shop, your whole palm wrapped around your mother's index finger, which smells of chlorine and onions. The shop is bigger than the city. You lean your head back. You look at the saleslady's flour-covered breasts. You feel the hair caressing your skin…

That fiend has not yet eaten the bun…

Not bun that yet eaten fiend…

You have not noticed that the teacher has been standing next to you for a long time and is moving her jaw irregularly and in sync with yours. You timidly stuff the bun in your pocket, quickly wipe your mouth, and say sorry. You always feel like someone is looking over your shoulder when you eat a bun, which is why you always eat in a panic and with a sense of shame. You hope that nobody you know turns up… He won't feel good that you're eating a bun, he will be upset… The raisins gather in your soft cheeks and they crunch one by one between your teeth… When will you enjoy this moment, this happiest but fleeting moment in life, where will it be?

It's like a stone

Don't touch it

Let it go

Don't touch it with your hand, dirty hand

dirty fingers…

It's his bun. It's his… what business is it of yours? You can't just take someone else's bun. It's a part of his body, like his hands and legs, his kidneys and skin. If you take it, you will cause him pain, you will kill him again, upset him… Maybe his mother put it in his pocket as he was leaving home this morning… What business is it of yours? You can't do that… Don't interfere in that mother-son relationship. But it is possible that he is the one who has found the time. He slipped away for a moment, stepped into the nearby shop, walked over to the baked goods section, bought my favorite raisin bun, put it in his pocket, and then felt embarrassed to eat it in public… You didn't know this, you scoundrels, but he knew, he *knew* that eating a raisin bun would not be appropriate in your presence, so he left it in his pocket and it went stale there.

Fine, don't touch it

I'm talking to you, leave it

Don't touch it, don't touch it, do not touch it…

You crazy parrot, who need this stale

Bun…

…Who needs a stale crazy bun… Who?

Perhaps a need his mother or father has, or his sister, or the man who works there with the sharp knives and ax. He's a skilled professional. An absolute cleanliness-loving guy. His tools turn into brushes in his hands. He says that this is an artform. But his masterpiece is removing bones from the ribcage. Have you seen it, how the chef cuts open fried chicken using scissors and skilfully separates the connecting tissues? And he is the chef of his own work. He improvises as he works, demonstratively closing his eyes, putting on some music, making coffee, making sure also to pour some for the people lying there. He lights a cigarette, takes in some drags and then stuffs it in their mouths and laughs. He loves having his picture taken with everyone and putting them in photoalbums labeled by the year. It will be interesting, you should check it out… but… but it's possible that that man will not eat the bun, he might put it in a bowl of water, soften it up, and he might then rip it up into small pieces and feed it to the sparrows, that have gone down in number these days… When you were small, sparrows were everywhere, like ants, and they would even survive the extremely cold winter months. Then they reduced in number, their population keeps decreasing… I wonder if it had crossed your mind in the morning that the bun would end up with the sparrows and that you would end up in a bed in this building, among the colorless and sad boats… You know, it crosses my mind, and almost every day, when I go past this building in my car, I sense something familiar, I want to imagine what the rooms look like, to feel the smell of meat coming from the walls, the uneven surface of the white spotted tiles, the lifeless and bland furniture, the shadows of insects running on the ceiling, the coarseness of the juicing equipment, the pointlessness of the draft blowing in from some unknown place and, finally, the crooked edges of the tin boats, the sky-blue paint peeling from their surfaces here and there… I want to feel the way the sharp, piercing and cutting instruments enter and leave my body, the weight of the electric saw… Sometimes, at night, when I wake up and leave the house unnoticed to buy bananas and cigars, I find myself at the gates of the building, surrounded by cats, and we gaze in one direction, always in that direction, at the window of the last room I occupied, where I will be alone, without my mother or father, without my clothes or Lilith… Seriously, I'm so scared, I don't want to feel alone when I'm in there… I would have liked for someone to be with me, even if it was the electrician from our neighborhood… But don't worry about it, even though we don't know each other, I'm with you now, I'm standing right next to you… I'm Aram… I'm going to celebrate my birthday in nineteen days, I'll invite you too, we'll go to a nice place, have something to drink, dance a little… we'll have cake… I won't invite too many people… it'll be just our crowd…

Are you crying?

You seem emotionally weak

That's okay, you'll learn

You're crying weak that's okay you'll learn emotionally

Look, look at his face… hey, hey… don't be scared, please take a quick look at his face, open your eyes and look… You see? Did you see? I told you he hadn't eaten it… Look under his eyes, you see? Right there, near the edge of his cheekbone, a large, black raisin is stuck there. I haven't seen a raisin that large in my life. Black, large, juicy. The fruitskin has cracked and abundant juice has flowed out, flooded his whole face, filled his mouth, stained his neck, spilled over his shoulder onto his sinewy arm, dyed his fingers, dripped from his nails to the tiles. The drops of dried blood at the edges of his nails are thin and delicate like spiderwebs. The cherry-colored thread sliding down his pinky finger has almost reached the tiles and hardened, as if it's the final thread of his life.

Congealed blood is tough to clean

Look at how the idiot's pinky is holding on to the tile

He kicks the thin thread and cuts it. The boy's pinky twitches. Your pinky twitches too. The wound on his face is extremely deep… I wonder if make-up will cover that hole? The edges of his mouth are layered in blue, his eyes are open, squinting with pain. I caress his hair such that nobody sees. Blood is dripping on my index finger. I raise my finger to my mouth and rub the drop against my tongue and palate. I swallow. The blood is semi-sweet. They say that your blood tastes like whatever you have had to drink in the morning. Ah… perhaps… I had had some semi-sweet coffee with Mother at dawn… Mother had been boasting that this was Columbian coffee and that she had bought it at the supermarket… Which one are you – the sixth, seventh or eighth? I don't know, but they are already driving me crazy, please tell them to go away, why can't they leave me alone? Mom has had that coffee ground especially for me but on one condition, that I don't leave home today…

I try to close his eyes, but his eyelids seem glued in place and do not move. We look at each other for the first and last time, with eyes that are hot and cold. I bring my lips to his ears and repeat my name, I tell him not to be afraid… He makes no sound, but his eyes grow softer.

See? He's wet himself before dying, like a woman

Like a dying woman see himself

His gray trousers are dark below his waist, pear-shaped, like the African continent… you were shy. When you wet yourself, you would cry the whole day because of that sense of guilt, you would go into the little house of boxes you had made yourself, and you would not come out… now what? Death is a sense of guilt…

After a burst of machine gun fire, when you would fall into those soft feathers, it is such a good feeling at first. Thousands of butterflies fill your head. You feel the flutter of their little wings. All the colors sparkle like the stars, then die out. The demonstrating protesters and the soldiers there seem taller than the plane trees nearby. You cannot see their heads. They were dancing. Spinning, spinning. Their hands writhing like a snake burning in a fire. The colors were running out. Suddenly, you see the Catholicos, who climbs the electric pole like a monkey, sits on top, and looks down beneath him. You're surprised – perhaps God convinced him to come and put an end to all this. Deep down you expect someone to come and punctuate this with a period, to send you home. But the Catholicos takes out his member like he was unsheathing a sword and starts urinating from that height… His urine is not yellowish, it's red and heavy… You feel a sharp, unbelievably powerful pain and you raise your palm to your left cheek… The heavy stream of blood causes your hand to shiver… You understand, but you need to convince yourself by putting your hand into your wound – the opening is broad and deep, you are overcome with misery… "Call an ambulance," "Please, quickly!" "Someone clamp down tight on this wound," "I can't feel a pulse…" Your senses are so heightened, you are slowly departing… with regret… you can feel your phone in your pocket… you haven't had the chance to reply to that new message… "Give him mouth-to-mouth," "Don't let him suffer any more, he's not breathing." But you're still here, you simply can't hear, or see, you don't know… You simply feel… You feel a wetness between your legs… Liquids are your last line of defense, they take the pain and the fear of solitude with them… That's all… Understand… You will no longer be…

At least all this one did was wet himself, that other guy had recalled a past lover in his death throes… I mean, what were they looking for? They got what they deserved, tomorrow their families would pay and that would be that… They would take them and hurl them into a pit, then eat *khash-lama* made from an old cow's meat at the memorial meal, and everyone would go back home…

Your phone rings. It's probably your mom, or your girlfriend, or your father, or your friends, or people that are concerned for your life, or it could be a wrong number, or… The phone keeps ringing. There will be no understanding of why you don't respond, of the indifference of your nonexistence… I think, how good would it be if you were to suddenly wake up from oblivion, pick up the phone, say "Hello, darling. Don't worry, I'll be there in an hour. Kisses," or "Mom, I'll be there soon, heat up the water so I can take a bath…" But you don't hear me, and you stubbornly refuse to answer the phone… Your face seems so familiar, almost like family, everyone knows everyone's face in our city. If you don't see a familiar face in a long time, then it will come to you in a dream and smile. Unfamiliar dead people come in your dreams, stand in front of you and smile quietly. You took it badly. Perhaps because that one was a boy your age.

Go out and get some fresh air, if you like.
It's just another corpse for me,
        you'll feel the same way soon.

                    ARAM PACHYAN

For you badly boy, feel out
            fresh air.

I'll stay with you a bit more… I said leave, I'll be out in a few minutes… I'll
be there soon… these are the final seconds… We are no longer going to
meet on the streets, on bus stops, in cafés, at your place or mine, because
you no longer exist… Since we're alone, I want to sing something for you,
but I don't have a good voice… I'll sing softly, okay… Why did they kill
you, why will they always kill you, why did the bullet ruin your pretty face,
why didn't they let you eat your raisin bun, why didn't they let you sleep
with your girlfriend at night, why am I talking while you are silent; I'm
embarrassed by your death, I'm embarrassed at the way I am standing…
how deep are these feelings lowered into the soil… lalalalalalala…. You
will no longer exist, you simply have to resign yourself to this, there is
no other way… The man living in this building will be talking with you
all along as he reaches into you and pulls out your internal organs, he'll
wash your abdominal cavity with water, fill you up with straw, use creams
to close that dark hole in your cheek, he will try to shut your mouth but
it won't work, he'll stick your skull together with super glue, he'll dress
you in a suit that's a couple sizes too big, he'll cut two toes off your right
foot so that he can put on your shoe, and he'll lay you down in a polished
coffin sent by the government, after which he'll say have a good journey,
and he won't forget about your last photograph… Can you imagine that,
little brother? A shiny, red coffin – with a comfortable, soft pillow, silk
sheets… They've brought it as a gift for you from Nar Dos Street… Could
you ever imagine that you would be going in such a luxurious coffin?
Your coffin is so big that a few million of us could have comfortably fit
inside, but nobody is going to come… I won't come either, because I'm
scared of not living… I'm sorry, but I really want to live, I really do… and
I want to live a loooong time… don't be angry… It won't be long before
you're forgotten, for sure, and that will make up for it, because people will
finally leave you alone and you can finally die in peace… church services,
lit candles… a constant sequence of formalities… but we both know that
God doesn't exist, there cannot be a God, because God cannot be a man,
there is no God, because God cannot be a God… it will be over quickly,
don't worry about it…

I take my hand to his pocket; the raisin bun is not there. I go through his pockets again. It's impossible, I had just seen it, it was there. I step out into the corridor. They are talking about a raise. He's holding the raisin bun and is tapping it on his knee. I walk up to him…

I need what you're holding

He looks at me like a cow

Why? Are you going to eat that corpse's bun?

Yes… give it to me

He tosses the bun with contempt. I catch it and go back into the room. I walk up to the boy and put the bun in his pocket, then lock the door from inside. The lights go out. The car's engine starts. The boy's phone rings, constantly, constantly… The car, sniffing the paved road like a rat, disappears into the darkness. The phone rings, constantly, constantly, constantly… They are going home… clump clump dump hump bump clump… and another bump… I fooled them, fooled… Those idiots think I'm with them… the phone rings… They think that I'm taking them home in my car… They think they're talking to me… But I have f o o l e d them, I've fooled them all, I'm not there, I'm not in the car… I was never there… I've hidden myself in the boy's pocket… with the bun…. Shhhhhhhhhh… don't tell anybody… nobody… please.

FATHER VILIK

There was a high-pitched voice every couple of seconds. "Perhaps there is someone under my bed, but who could it be? I live with my father, and my taps are tightly shut." I felt my way through the room in the darkness and walked up to the window. There was silence. The platform in the courtyard was deserted. The electric lamp hanging from the roof, melted here and there, was lit in solitude through a crooked wire. That lamp had never been switched off from the day it had been installed. There was a backgammon board on the table and cards for belote. The voice was heard again. I broke out in sweat. The voice was coming from the platform side. I took a cola from the fridge and drank it greedily. My throat constricted, it was very cold. I sat down on the wooden chair and leaned my back to the railing. The crackling of the bubbles that could be heard from the cola distracted me for a moment, then I heard that now-familiar voice in the distance again. It was like a child crying now, a child crying, a cat mewing, high-pitched, high-pitched, quiet. My hands and legs had gone numb, I wasn't feeling well. My father moved in bed and let out a snore. I swayed as I walked into his room. The smell of vodka was so strong that my head grew heavy at once. He was splayed on the king-sized bed, without a sheet, one leg was half-bent, his lips glued together, foaming. I touched his knee lightly with four fingers, he snored briefly and turned to the other side. What should I do? I decided to say something.

"Dad."

"…"

"Dad."

He was fighting in his sleep, not reacting. I had to talk, at once. I started to poke his body powerfully, he opened his eyes a bit and it was like he was looking at me but could not see.

"Dad…"

"Fuck you…"

"Dad, can you hear me?"

"Do you know who I am?"

He was probably having a dream.

"Dad…"

"Weigh three kilos of that…"

"I don't feel good," my voice went hoarse.

I left the bedroom. There was silence. I wanted to suppress my laughter, but I began to giggle to myself (I'll tell you why later), I had practiced this, my whole body would seize up, and I would lean against a wall, clench my fists, and die of laughter. Once in a while, when my heart beat fast, a high-pitched whistle would slip through my lips, very softly. "This is the sound that woke me."

When I calmed down, I dressed up, picked up a paper and pencil, and began to write.

They don't understand me because I really want them to underatand… I felt like having some vegetables yesterday, but I ate meat… I write on some paper every day, "I'm quitting my job, I'm not going back tomorrow… I can't make any friends, I don't know why I upset everyone… Nothing makes me happy… I hate myself and I hate everyone, I always want to do bad things… I miss your tongue, your skin, your Valerian smell, your yellow face, your cat… I was eating an apple yesterday, it felt bitter in my mouth, I was chewing the worm insi…" The pencil broke. I tried to sharpen it with a knife, but it didn't work, the knife was blunt, half of its handle broke. That knife had been a gift to my mother on March 8, Women's Day, from someone I can't remember.

I threw the paper aside; it was already light outside. I made my father a cup of strong, bitter coffee. I boiled it well, several times. That's how he liked it. He barely got up, his face swollen.

"Hi, little guy…"

"Hello."

"Well, bring the coffee…"

He swallowed the coffee in one go, then got dressed, took some money out of his pocket, put it on the table, cumbersomely left and closed the door. I had decided for sure, although that decision had ripened to an extent that it seemed to exist outside my body. I tied my tie around a doll's neck, put on my flowery shirt and left the house. It was very hot. I walked downtown. At a slow pace, I stepped around people, streets, trees, cars, and the noise; you could tell where I was going from my steps. I walked up to the church. There was silence. Coolness. I walked in, making an awkward sign of the cross. I went up to the candle seller. She was a very old woman, a virgin with the cunning face of a salesperson, but pretending to be serious, as if the work that she was doing pleased God.

"Give me a candle," I said, my head hung low.

"How many?"

"One."

She gave me a candle but when I picked it up, she waited, the wrinkles on her face multiplied, and she did not fully let go.

"Where's the money, son?"

"I don't have any," I was angry.

"No candle, in that case."

She tried to pull it back, but I had grabbed it tightly with my fingers. The orange candle crumbled in my palm. The woman darkened and began to pour curses on me, she was even asking someone to call the police, though there was nobody around. I wanted to kill the old woman then and there, it would have been the only logical way out, but I did not have an ax or a knife in my hand, just the candle, and you can't kill someone with that. She was talking, shouting, singing hymns, saying God have mercy, asking the Lord for forgiveness in my stead. It was a good thing we were the only people in the church at that moment – me, the old woman, and that maddening voice of hers…

"Hripsime, what's going on?" a new voice appeared, that of a man.

I turned around. It was a priest, of medium height, with a long, black, shiny, cassock. He looked like a young crow, his face was hidden by a dense brown beard, the hairs on his chin were spotted with white, as if they were snowflakes. "I wonder how he eats?" I wondered. "He would barely be able to find his own mouth in there." His eyes were large, watery, red capillaries darting about in the whites. His pupils were slowly dilating, they were calm and exploring. The woman grew calm at the priest's voice.

"Holy father, this son of evil will not pay for his candle, what should I do?" Then she suddenly grabbed her back and began to complain of arthritis, blaming me for her pain…

The priest took out a candle from the drawer and silently held it out to me, but I did not take it. I turned around and went to sit down at a pew, they had hurt my feelings. I didn't know why I had come here. I really did not know. Sometimes you just end up coming to a church – you're tired of home, cafés, restaurants. I sat for a long time, my butt hurt but the wood of the pew was pleasant, I was looking for smoothed knots on its surface, thought I had found one, and I counted the rings in it. Some time later, I noticed that I had been left alone. It was getting dark. The candle seller was cursing me from the corner of her eye as she adjusted her headscarf. Then the pew creaked again.

"The church is closing, son," the priest's shy voice said without confidence.

"I'm sitting here."

The priest did not move. "Is he praying to himself?" I had gone numb as I thought, "They must have called from the office and said that I had not shown up for work today. He's going to kill me, there's no point going home."

"Are you feeling unwell?" The priest's voice trembled. "Do you want to talk a little?"

"Talk about what? There's nothing to talk about," I grew angry.

"God is all-powerful, son."

"I don't believe in God. I've come here to look at this waxy tuff stone, they say it's good for one's health…"

"That's good. I'm Vilik," he held out his hand.

"Aram," I shot back without holding out mine, then I attacked, "You're in church from morning to evening, you already know all your regular visitors, the blind and tired beggars in the streets bow their heads when they see you, they kiss the ends of your cossack. Yes, your tunic smells of incense."

I was quiet all of a sudden.

"I live right behind the church. Let's go together, my wife has made dinner."

I went. I felt a fit of laughter coming again. But I had to keep it down because I had once been beaten by a cop and a tooth had broken, my upper lip had gone beet red. I had been walking along Saryan Street when I saw a little boy that was biting into a piece of watermelon he had been holding with both hands. At that moment, his life began and ended with that piece of watermelon. The world was a watermelon to him, emotional and tasty, he was eating with such diligence and relish that I felt like laughing. I had burst out. A cop appeared before me at that very moment. He took out a piece of paper and pen from his pocket, cleared his throat and addressed me:

"You get a ticket for laughing, we have a new law in our country that prohibits laughing out loud. You can only laugh to yourself, if you want, and that too only at home. You have to be punished for this infraction now – according to the law in our country, I have to break your front tooth for this public display of loud laughter." As soon as he said that he took out a wooden club from his belt and used its blunt end to strike my mouth a powerful blow. My tooth broke. While I was moaning with pain, the policeman filled out a detailed report. He gave me the stub, wished me well, and said a warm goodbye.

Father Vilik's house was like a little cellar where one could store canned food for the winter. There were a few items in the house – a table, chairs, bookshelf, clock, and bed. The clock clicked as it worked, I thought that it must be an unpleasant thing to hear at night. The washroom and toilet were outside. A middle-aged woman was there to greet us.

"Suzy, this is a friend of mine – Aram."

"Pleased to meet you, I'm Suzy." She got up and brought us a couple of chairs. We sat down. Suzy had a soft voice. I did not pay much attention to her face, but she was very beautiful.

Father Vilik took out some money from his pocket and put it on the table.

"Just one baptism today, Suze, but that's okay, at least it's something. So, what have you cooked today?"

Suzy blushed, she was probably embarrassed. She brought some fried vegetables, bread, and wine. She sat down next to us. I ate nothing. Father Vilik and Suzy felt bad.

"Consider us your friends, Aram *jan*, we are ready to help you if there's anything we can do," he said.

I felt that Vilik loved his wife very much because his long fingers were caressing the curve of her left shoulder blade. I told them everything. I said that I had not gone to work today. I was afraid to go back home. If my father had found out, he would not let me in. Then I went quiet and picked up some vegetables with my fork.

"Bring me my sneakers, Suzy," Vilik said, "You get ready too, we're going out." But he did not say where. Vilik left. He returned a short while later wearing different clothes. He was wearing a T-shirt that said "With Love" on it in English, and purple trousers. Father Vilik called a cab.

"Let's go."

The three of us stepped outside and got into the taxi.

"What's your address?" Vilik asked softly.

"The Vegetable Market District…"

"Driver, take us to the Vegetable Market District…"

And we were off, going to our house – Father Vilik, Suzy, and me… Vilik stopped the car on the way and bought some semi-sweet wine. We arrived. I was trembling. We stopped near the door of our house. I rang the bell. There were strange sounds coming from inside. The door opened. My father's eyes were blurred. He was barely holding on to the door. My father did not have trousers on.

"You son of a bitch… You've qu-quit your job, have you?"

"So they've called and told him." I shrunk.

"Hello, my name is Vilik. I'm a friend of Aram's. How are you?"

My father almost fell over, but Father Vilik did not let that happen. He held on to his arm as if he were a family member.

"Have you read any Jack London?" my father abruptly asked Vilik…

"Yes, *The Sea-Wolf*…"

"Oh my, are you serious? That's great! Do you know Wolf Larsen? I'm a Wolf Larsen kinda guy, come right in… Aram *jan*, why aren't you inviting them in? Come in, come in." My father was falling over again, but Father Vilik was by his side. We sat down. I was setting the table. Vilik took out the wine. My father liked that very much. He grabbed him and kissed his cheek. Suzy came to help me, she cut some tomatoes and cucumbers and put them on the table. I noticed that she used a technique for cutting the tomatoes that did not let any of the juice out. As they moved, her tiny, delicate fingers were almost transparent. We filled our cups. My father proposed a toast. "I'm very happy to have you here, Vilik *jan*. Very happy that you are friends of my Aram," my father turned to me, "So you've quite your job, you son of a bitch?"

"That's okay, he'll find another job," Father Vilik came to my rescue.

"Well, Vilik *jan*, if you've read Jack London, then you're a friend of mine…"

We drank. We ate. My father told Vilik that he was a surgeon, that he had been there throughout the war, he had helped people… He must have repeated that a thousand times, I helped people, Vil, I helped people, Vil, I saved people, Vil, I operated on wounded children, Vil, I removed their arms, deformed from the shelling, Vil, I love children, Vil, I love their amputated hands, Vil, I love people, Vil, I love life, Vil, I feel so alone, Vil, I feel great, Vil, I love you, Vil, I love this idiot, Vil, my Aram has no friends, Vil, don't leave him, Vil, I want to operate on you, Vil, come to the hospital tomorrow, Vil, please, Vil, it would be my pleasure to operate on you, Vil… And after each word, Father Vilik would bless my father, he even agreed to sacrifice one of his organs and undergo surgery at his hands. Then my father turned to me and reprimanded me for not offering Suzy anything to eat. Some time later, my father, Vilik and Suzy were singing a song by Sayat Nova. I was so amused I lost my head. I stepped out into the corridor and began running here and there. I changed my shoes and ran out of the house. I flew down the staircase into the courtyard; there was nobody there. I saw three cats lined up next to the garbage bin, then I turned back. The sun was coming up. My father had fallen asleep in his chair. Suzy covered him with a sheet. We called a taxi. I went out to see them off.

"Aram, I've very… very happy… *jan*, that… goodbye, see you around…"

Father Vilik kissed my forehead. I took out an old lilac from the flower-pot and gave it to Suzy. She was very happy. She said goodbye to me with her delicate fingers. The taxi left. Suzy had leaned her head on Father Vilik's shoulder. Some loud laughter had been heard in the Vegetable Market District that day.

The next morning, my father and I did not wake up.

NIGHT UNDER
THE SHADOW

When the boy opened his eyes in the morning, the nightingale's head was missing. He put his hand in the cage, took out the stiff bird and started to lick the body that had separated from the head. The bird's blood was sweet and warm. He carefully examined the area around the cage but could not find the head. His mother was asleep in the adjacent bed. Her white thigh had slipped out from under the covers. He slid down from his bed somehow, approached his mother, and ran his little fingers along her velvety skin that was like peach fuzz. He had seen his mother carefully shaving her soapy legs in the bathroom once, after which she had applied some lotion that smelled like sour cream. He liked to rub his cheek along his mother's smooth, clean skin like a cat, and this was different to how touching his father's face would hurt him. He quietly picked up the edge of the sheet and covered his mother's thigh before returning to bed. He licked the blood clean off the nightingale's feathers, took a fine-toothed comb from the drawer, and meticulously groomed them. Then he walked up to the window, pocketed a few feathers plucked from the creature's little wings, and threw the bird out.

Has it escaped? Did you open the cage door? His mother walked about the hospital room anxiously that morning, bending over and looking for the nightingale under the bed, asking the jaundiced children whether they had noticed her son's bird. The boy in the far bed of the room said that he had seen it at night. He had sad, blue eyes and frail facial features; he was almost always asleep in bed. They had brought the child in critical condition, his body was exteremely feeble and wasted at first. However, even after he had recovered considerably, he still did not leave his bed and would respond to the doctor's questions with difficulty, before suddenly spitting on his hand

and kicking at him. On the windowsill? Was it trying to fly out the window? No, it was calling out for help. The boy fell silent and turned sadly to the wall.

The boys would hush down when the creaking of the nurse's trolley would be heard. Yet another injection that would bring the daily wave of tragic crying and wild resistance. Only two people were not bothered by the injections. At first, the nurse even gained pleasure from doing it. When the needle slid under his skin, she looked with surprise at the boy whose facial muscles had not even twitched. At the moment of the injection, the other boy would also fixate his wandering gaze at the nightingale's empty cage and ignore the needle going in and out. Once, the nurse had intentionally caused the boy pain, but he had simply turned his head and looked softly into her eyes; the nurse had looked away, a kind of lifeless evil was shining in those eyes.

At night, he took out the nightingale's head and examined its orange beak under the moonlight for a long time. Then he inspected its little black eyes with the tips of his fingers. They were cold and slippery, like glass. The boy began to sob and stuck his head under the bedsheets so that his voice would not be heard. Some time later, his tears subsided by themselves. Drying his eyes on the sheets, he got out of bed, felt the floor with his feet, found his mother's huge slippers, put them on, and silently walked through the passage separating the two beds. In his dream, the unbelievably huge nightingale head had been hopping along the hospital room ceiling. He opened his eyes in a panic. His sweat-drenched shirt had glued itself to his back, he wanted to call out to his mother but then changed his mind and took out the bird's head. Its beak and eyes were gone. He tried to swallow the head but could not, it was too big. He took it out of his mouth and put it in his pocket. Putting on his mother's slippers, he walked to the window, opened it silently, and threw out the head.

The children, getting healthier every day, were noisy, running about, pushing each other around, exchanging toys, laughing, moving their beds here and there. The boys located in the two ends of the room never participated in these games. They would turn around once in a while and stare at each other, then turn back to face their walls. Why don't you talk, why don't you say something to the other children? His mother would worry. Don't be sad, we'll get you a new nightingale. No, I don't want another one. During the day, his mother would convince him to leave his bed, and she would take him out, help him walk in the corridor, but the boy would get bored quickly and would return to bed. He hated all the noisy children, whose laughter made him forget the dreams he had at night.

His mother slept so soundly that she did not feel the fly walking on her nose. He stood next to her head and looked at the frills in her nightgown, which caused him unbearable embarrassment. At night, he always wanted to squish or punch his mother's belly, and he was only just barely able to suppress that desire burning in his soul. His leg would stop at the very last moment. He would think, why are Mother's feet so big and why were Father's feet so small? Why are Mother's feet like the huge fish that are sold in the market? Every day at dawn, he would worriedly rub his own feet, panicking that they would someday turn into fish and start fluttering about.

From under the bedsheet, the boy took out a large butterfly he had killed on the windowsill the previous evening. It was more of a forest moth – ugly, almost black. Its wings had several brown spots and melon-shaped dense droplets, while its hairy body was grey and wrinkly. He walked up barefooted to the nightingale's cage this time, opened the door, and put the butterfly inside, then turned around and looked at the boy's mother. She was pretty and her nightgown did not have any frills.

The boy opened his eyes and saw a silhouette lit by the rays of dawn. "The nightingale has returned." But when that green haze dissipated, he realized that it was a butterfly lying in the cage. He took out the butterfly, cuddled it and took it with him to bed.

His father, standing in the shadow of a watermelon, looked at the window of the hospital room. Your father wants to see you, come closer, you're getting on my nerves. The boy was not listening to his mother. He whispered as he counted the moles on her face – there were seven. Some of them had short or long hairs on their surface, others were only slightly different from freckles and appeared only when his mother would sigh and puff her cheeks. Don't you understand? He's come to see you, get up, she continued. His father grew tired of waiting so long, the staff at the reception had refused to allow the watermelon. Through the mist reflected on the window, he saw his father's vanishing back and, below his shoulder, that long, coarse arm, which often left a mark on his mother's left cheek…

The children were afraid of the dark, they would ask the adults to keep the hospital room lights switched on until they fell asleep, but he could give shape to all the thoughts in his head only in the darkness. The swelling in his liver was gradually subsiding. You could see that by the egg-shaped shadow he cast on the wall, which slowly grew smaller. He would play with the shadows of sick children all day, fight with them. The shadows were cunning, they would never make a noise. They would leap out of unexpected places, slither like snakes over legs and slide over shoulders, wrap themselves around necks and caress cheeks, turn into massive breasts, ice cream, naughty mice. He would try to catch that moment each time and kiss one of them passionately, but shadows were sudden and rapid in their movements. They would adroitly pull back and pour into the boy's hair, wet it, slam against the railing, and dissipate. Their star-shaped shards would fall to the floor, seep into it, stagnate, and fill the whole space of the room. He picked up the plucked wings of the butterfly off his chest and rubbed them between his thumb and forefinger. They were as thin and weak as paper towels. The boy swayed as he stepped out of bed. His mother was asleep on her stomach this time, half her face covered by her messy hair. A bunch of it had fallen on her half-open lips and fluttered with her warm and weak breathing. That night, his mother had put on her favorite white nightgown, the one without the threaded embroidery, the one that emphasized the whole charm and fragility of her body, those waves of curves, her smooth skin, the untouchable softness of her recesses, the solitude of her tense shoulders, the shyness of her sensitive breasts. At home, he would secretly hug his mother's white nightgown, kiss it, breathe in its smell into his lungs, place it on the couch and straighten its folds. He would think of the nightgown as his mother's skin and her only protector. When his mother and father went to sleep, he would cry all night for his mother and squeeze the handle of the kitchen knife he kept hidden beneath his pillow, imagining how her delicate body was bent below his father's disgusting, huge bones, how he used his dirty, coarse hands to remove his mother's nightgown and fondle her body, how his hairy legs would scrape and bloody her skin. The boy would be surprised and feel sorry for every night his mother spent, placing all his hope on her white nightgown. When they sat in the red streetcar or walked in the city, he would search in the crowd for a man that could replace his father, looking mainly at their fingers. If they were long and thinly boned, with semi-swarthy skin and no tense twitches, they would get the boy's approval. He felt that such fingers could never hurt his mother, they would softly bury themselves in her body and love all its layers. The boy would let out a deep sigh.

His thighs grew wet. The urine flowed down into his slippers and poured onto the floor. He lowered the butterfly wings slowly onto his mother's back and looked upward. The large shadow they cast on the ceiling created a terrifying image that swallowed the last bluish ray of light. There was real silence in the hospital room now. From under his pillow, the boy removed the long-barelled guns with engraved handles and used his mother's handkerchief to polish each of the barrels in turn. Content with his work a little while later, he carefully made his bed, put the handkerchief in place and walked along the room. Reaching the boy's bed, he quietly sat down, holding the guns tightly in both his hands. Are you asleep? No, I was waiting for you. Your father had come yesterday and brought a watermelon, did you see him? Yes, I saw him. How could you have if I was the only one standing near the window? I was behind you. Does he hit you? No, he hits my mother. Why? My father has wiry hair like you. Like me? Yes, his hair can't be combed. Have you already made your bed? I'll be done in a minute.

His blue eyes lit up their path. The boys left the hospital room and walked down the winding staircase. The guard was asleep and did not notice the boys leaving the main hospital door. The cold autumn wind and abundant flow of oxygen immediately woke up their numb bodies. Their long nightgowns gave the boys the appearance of white ghosts, floating along with the wind without touching the ground. There was a light drizzle. They walked into a narrow street, entered the park opposite and walked on a path. The drops of rain had gathered in the bent leaves and flowed down in streams on the boys' heads and shoulders. They were completely drenched. On the way, he stopped and took off his slippers. Let's stamp on the leaves on the ground while we walk, he said. The boy hesitated for a moment but could not resist the temptation and took off his large slippers, running after his friend. With joyful exclamations, they trampled on all the leaves they could see and ran along new paths, sinking happily into the soil, picking up handfuls of it and rubbing it on their milky bodies, opening their mouths before shaking tree branches and drinking the flowing rainwater, falling, rising, shaking their hands, rubbing them against tree trunks. Soon, they arrived at an opening and fell silent.

The raindrops flowed to the ends of their hair, the lengths of their brows, the space between their eyelashes, and then fell back, crashing into the grass. The drops of sweat that had formed from their joy rested on their reddened cheeks and warmed them. If I have a scratch on my leg, you'll be the first to fire, if you have a scratch on your leg, the first shot will be mine. They raised their nightgowns. The boy had a thin, bloodless scratch with smooth edges, caused by a tree branch. They stood in the center of the field, turned their backs to each other, and started to walk, counting each step loudly as they paced. Their voices kept growing apart and soon could not be heard.

He turned around and tried to find the white folds of the other's nightgown in the darkness, but he could only make out some flickering in the distance, as if someone was using a lantern to give signals. He held out the gun, put his finger on the trigger and tried to aim at one of the sparks he saw far away. His hand trembled. He brought up his other hand and fully embraced the handle of the gun, but then he suddenly started to fall. As he fell, all he heard was the dull thundering of a gun and the happy splash of a fountain from his forehead.

He ran up and stood over the boy. The black pupils of his open eyes dilated and covered the whites, looking like a nightingale's eyes. He bent over and closed the boy's eyelids using a forefinger, then picked up the gun lying in the grass and used both his hands to turn it around and face the child. He took out the butterfly wings from his pocket, placed them on his back, and looked upward. He had never seen such a large shadow.

WHERE ARE YOU, LYOV?

When weakness finally dominates inside and out,
Then your healing hand becomes a necessity,
And when life is fully succumbing in all parts of the human spirit,
Help is always needed there because there is nothing else...
Grigor Narekatsi, *Book of Lamentations*

Where are you, Lyov?

I have been searching for you for three weeks. I come here and I freeze like a rock in the empty space where your books used to be carefully piled. Where are those banana boxes that used to fill up this empty space? Those old, torn boxes with the tags "Bonanzal" and "Adria" in which you were supposed to carry bananas, but which you used to hold books instead. Your boxes were falling apart because you were one of the first book salesmen that arrived at the Vernissage. Maybe you just burned those boxes to warm yourself up during those cold days, or maybe you just threw them away. I remember how you used to dig up a fantastic plastic bag from between the books in those boxes. I had never seen such unbelievable bags – all of them completely ragged, oily, with dried crumbs of *khachapuri* still in them, soily, misshapen, and with holes. We used to lose a half-hour of our lives until we would find the opening of the bag through joint efforts and stick the book that I bought from you inside. Everytime, I would try to tell you that I didn't need a bag, but you would be stubborn as a mule and force me, saying "Books must enter the house in a bag," and then you would excitedly search for your next big discovery. I would give in at that point, but as soon as I crossed the street, I would throw away the bag in the closest trash can so I could free the book from your latest presence...

On the weekends, whenever I pass the Vernissage by car, I glance your way with a trembling heart. I don't see you, Lyov. The other book salesmen, whom you never liked much, are always at their usual spots. They are getting more and more books, while the banana boxes are being piled up into pyramids. I know that will upset you and you will have a new reason to light a cigarette and cough in fits.

Lyov, I think that empty space doesn't symbolize spacelessness or lifelessness, it is an unending sadness, an exclusive opportunity to rediscover the past. No one can fill the space you have emptied because no human life could be replaced by another... I dream of saving you, of gathering your pieces, making my memory a path by which you can return...

Your footprints can no longer be noticed in the space you emptied. The snow has melted, making a map of the asphalt in some spots. A banana skin is lying between two puddles, like a naked, crouching girl. Do you remember, whenever a beautiful girl used to walk by your books, you used to wink at me with a soft look and whisper in my ear, "Enough getting lost in books! Look, what a girl! Go after her right now and marry her!" Beauty had an immediate impact on your soul. You were an ordinary person who extraordinarily valued beauty because you were beautiful too – dreamy in a way, you moved softly, you were calm, and you had polished speech. The pupils of your eyes had the color of spring grass and they used to surge with every word that came out of your mouth...

I am looking closely at the banana skin, I mean the girl, who is lying inside you sadly. I think she is going to die today, she won't survive the cold tonight, and perhaps it will rain in the morning and damage her fragile body. But that's all right, I am calm in any case. The girl will die in your arms. She will melt inside you, and perhaps she will warm you a little... But what happened? You have never been absent this long. Maybe you have the flu or maybe it's your sick lungs again. It had crossed my mind that you had tuberculosis, you used to cough so badly, the ringing sound of your lungs could be heard all the way to Komitas Street. I would avoid shaking your hand hello. I used to shiver when I felt the dampness of your hand in my palm. I used to wash my hands for a long time at home using different soaps and my father's surgical sanitizers, seriously worried about your immortal bacteria. However, the feeling of your palm never leaves me; I suddenly feel its moist presence during the day. I don't ask your bookseller friends about you. I am afraid that one of them will hiccup and say what I expect to hear – "Lyov is dead." Although I guess after I hear the news, I will still keep walking around the Vernissage and imagine your poor tombstone in a completely random place, lost among a slough of rough soil and pits. It's all right, Lyov, you would fit comfortably in a half-square too. A twig stuck on your tomb above your head, reminiscent of the cross's predecessor, would cause a snicker. From the very first day we met, I was waiting for your death because you were not doing well at all, you had no money for bread, you were slowly dying of starvation, you used to mutter that you were a Ph.D. candidate once. But your science was your books, Lyov. Books were your life's adventure…

As always, I owe you money, you probably remember. What can I do? You are the one who, with bowed head, told me in your muffled voice, "Take it, pay me when you have the money." But I knew, Lyov, I knew that you needed the money that very moment just like water and air. Your eyes were wet from the tears you held back. That moment you were bent over like a chess knight. I can't forget the day when you were begging me to buy a book from you, but I was tired of your pleading and just turned around and walked down the street. You followed me, you staggered after me with your miserable and helpless gait, holding out the book in your hand, as if you were a plastic bag blowing in the wind. You weren't calling out my name anymore. You were mute. I was ignoring you. Soon, I stopped by the last bookseller on the corner of the street. I chose a book and purchased it right before your eyes, then I turned around and stared hard at your face. You were no longer in this world. Only your black coat and your tweed hat remained of you. I kept walking. I crossed the street. Your shadow followed me. I walked very fast to the trash can, ripped the book apart, and threw it inside, then turned around and yelled, "Enough! Leave me alone, Lyov! What do you want from me? Leave me alone…" I ran to the subway, looking back every so often. You kept coming with the book under your arm, Lyov, like inevitable death. And I knew, I knew what I was running away from. I was running away from the fear of sharing the same fate. But suddenly I was rooted to my spot. You came up right beside me. Your lungs were shaking like a broken engine. You took the box of Chibookh cigarettes out of your pocket and asked, "Smoke?" I didn't reject you. We smoked quietly. We stood for a long time. Then we smoked again. For a moment, we smiled. I tried to walk away quietly. Your hand tapped my shoulder. I turned around. You offered the book again. "Take it. Pay me when you have the money." I took the book because I had no other choice. I haven't paid you back yet. I think it was 500 drams.

Lyov, I am afraid of you, I am afraid that your fate will recur. You know that I am good for nothing. My dad gives me money sometimes. You probably know my dad. The two of you are very alike – you have that same kind and undemanding smile. My father is ill just like you, Lyov. I await his death with terror every second, just like I waited for yours... When my dad is gone, I will be an absolute bum. I'll die of starvation. But before that happens, I'll probably sell all the books on my shelves, just like you. I have decided, Lyov. I am going to pile my books in your very spot, all lined up in banana boxes. I am going to sell all of them, every last one, until all my shelves are empty. And I am not going to have anything else in this life. Then a young man will appear and examine my last book… he will not buy it, he will not pay attention to my pleas. And I will walk after him just like you, holding the book tightly under my arm. I will walk and I will turn into a grain of dust and I will never reach him.

I am a little better now. My friends are helping me. If we meet one day, I'll tell you all about them for sure. All of them love books, just like you. But will we meet someday day, Lyov? I don't know. I am very worried. I don't remember where your live. I was there once, with a friend. It was a very plain, cold house, like I was in the potato eaters' world. Your bookshelves were almost completely empty, which meant that your life was ending… That day I chose several books. I didn't want to buy the last books that were left on your shelves because I wanted you to live; I wanted you to live for the beautiful little girl that I saw in your house, sitting obediently on a wooden chair. She kept smiling. I think your daughter was sick, Lyov. I wonder how the poor child is doing now. I remember how she got off her chair and came right up to me, smiling; perhaps she wanted a chocolate, but I was looking for books again like some kind of beast. Your warm smile flickered on your daughter's face. I saw her in a dream once with her round, smiling face, that same summer hat covering her bald head. She rested her face on mine and her chubby fingers played with my nose and lips… How I want you to be alive, Lyov… I want to see the child, I want to buy some chocolate and a stuffed animal for her, to gently touch her summer hat… How I want you to fill up your space in the Vernissage, all several square meters of it, with books, arranging your boxes… How I want to see your black coat and your tweed hat from afar, I want to breathe in the suffocating smoke of your Chibookh cigarette… I want to hear the echoing ring of your sick lungs, to return your 500 drams… And do you know how I want to meet you? I want to stand behind you like an unexpected, colorless shadow and tap the sleeve of your coat, so that when you turn around, I scream with ucontrollable joy, "WHERE WERE YOU, LYOV?"

Goodbye, Bird

by Aram Pachyan

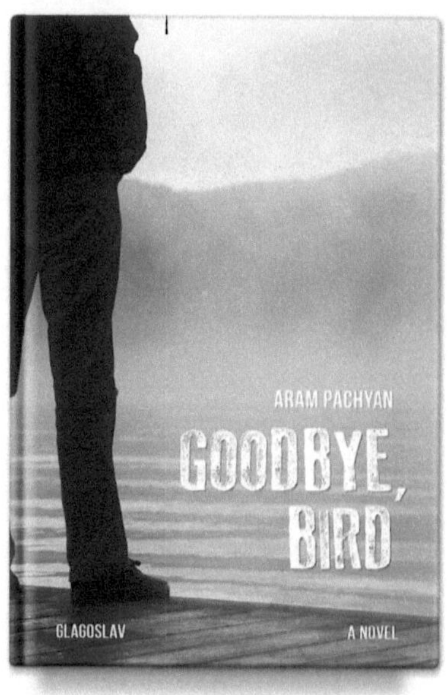

For a twenty-eight-year-old young man who returned from the army several years ago but has yet to reacclimatize to ordinary life, every step, gesture, word, and vision is a revelation, which takes him back to the beginning, to a time when reality had lost its shape, and turned into a new and imperceptible world. In his imagination, he embodies a number of different characters, he feels the presence of his girlfriend again, and remembers friends from his childhood and from the army, who are now gone. This is a book of questions, and the answers to these questions are to be found by the reader. The novel is like a puzzle which needs to be pieced together, and the picture is not complete until the last piece is in place, until the last word of the book has been read.

This book was published with the support of the Ministry of Culture of the Republic of Armenia under the "Armenian Literature in Translation" Program.

Buy it > www.glagoslav.com

The Door was Open
by Karine Khodikyan

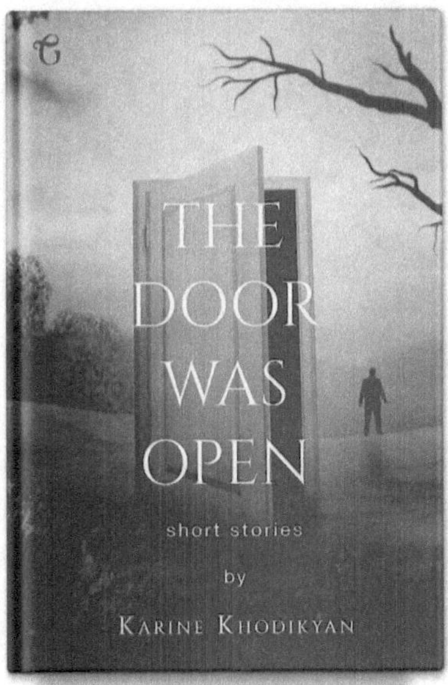

The short fiction of Karine Khodikyan can be described as intellectual fiction for women. These short stories with a "mystical touch" tell stories about women – young and old, happy and sad; even when the protagonist is not a woman, the story will immerse you into the life of a woman, revealing her role in anything and everything.

This book was published with the support of the Ministry of Culture of the Republic of Armenia under the "Armenian Literature in Translation" Program.

Buy it > www.glagoslav.com

Jesus' Cat

by Grig

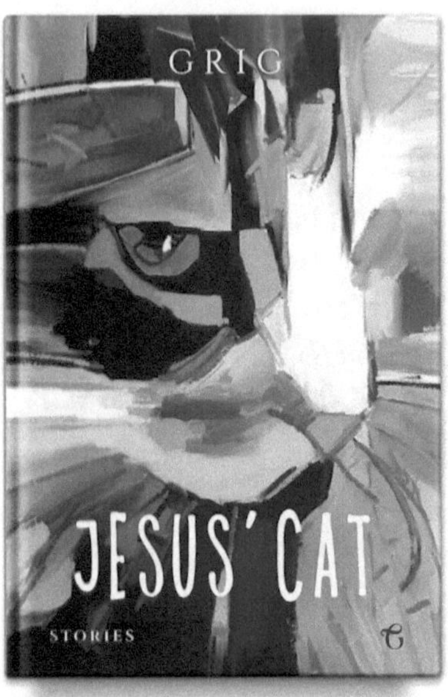

Jesus' Cat is the first book by this young prose writer. The stories involved in this collection reveal, on the one hand, a unique writing style, and on the other, an original perspective on the world and people. This combination allows characters to develop in Grig's creative space that helps readers discover another invisible side of life.

This book was published with the support of the Ministry of Culture of the Republic of Armenia under the "Armenian Literature in Translation" Program.

Buy it > www.glagoslav.com

Ravens before Noah

by Susanna Harutyunyan

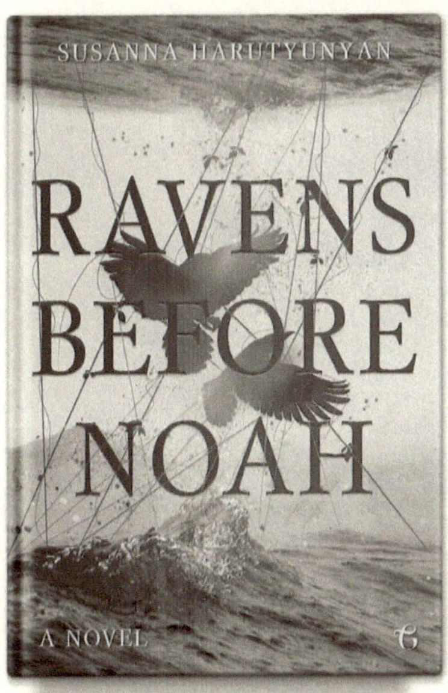

This novel is set in the Armenian mountains sometime in 1915-1960. An old man and a new born baby boy escape from the Hamidian massacres in Turkey in 1894 and hide themselves in the ruins of a demolished and abandoned village. The village soon becomes a shelter for many others, who flee from problems with the law, their families, or their past lives. The villagers survive in this secret shelter, cut off from the rest of the world, by selling or bartering their agricultural products in the villages beneath the mountain.

Years pass by, and the child saved by the old man grows into a young man, Harout. He falls for a beautiful girl who arrived in the village after being tortured by Turkish soldiers. She is pregnant and the old women of the village want to kill the twin baby girls as soon as they are born, to wash away the shame…

Buy it > www.glagoslav.com

Olanda

by Rafał Wojasiński

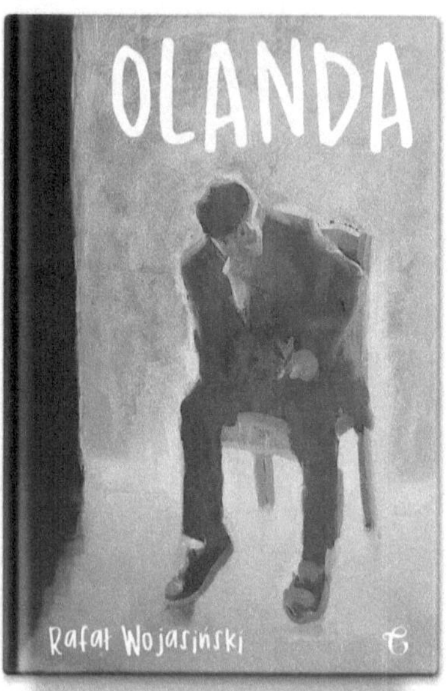

I've been happy since the morning. Delighted, even. Everything seems so splendidly transient to me. That dust, from which thou art and unto which thou shalt return — it tempts me. And that's why I wander about these roads, these woods, among the nearby houses, from which waft the aromas of fried pork chops, chicken soup, fish, diapers, steamed potatoes for the pigs; I lose my eye-sight, and regain it again. I don't know what life is, Ola, but I'm holding on to it. Thus speaks the narrator of Rafał Wojasiński's novel *Olanda*. Awarded the prestigious Marek Nowakowski Prize for 2019, *Olanda* introduces us to a world we glimpse only through the window of our train, as we hurry from one important city to another: a provincial world of dilapidated farmhouses and sagging apartment blocks, overgrown cemeteries and village drunks; a world seemingly abandoned by God — and yet full of the basic human joy of life itself.

Buy it > www.glagoslav.com

Glagoslav Publications Catalogue

- *The Time of Women* by Elena Chizhova
- *Andrei Tarkovsky: The Collector of Dreams* by Layla Alexander-Garrett
- *Andrei Tarkovsky - A Life on the Cross* by Lyudmila Boyadzhieva
- *Sin* by Zakhar Prilepin
- *Hardly Ever Otherwise* by Maria Matios
- *Khatyn* by Ales Adamovich
- *The Lost Button* by Irene Rozdobudko
- *Christened with Crosses* by Eduard Kochergin
- *The Vital Needs of the Dead* by Igor Sakhnovsky
- *The Sarabande of Sara's Band* by Larysa Denysenko
- *A Poet and Bin Laden* by Hamid Ismailov
- *Watching The Russians (Dutch Edition)* by Maria Konyukova
- *Kobzar* by Taras Shevchenko
- *The Stone Bridge* by Alexander Terekhov
- *Moryak* by Lee Mandel
- *King Stakh's Wild Hunt* by Uladzimir Karatkevich
- *The Hawks of Peace* by Dmitry Rogozin
- *Harlequin's Costume* by Leonid Yuzefovich
- *Depeche Mode* by Serhii Zhadan
- *The Grand Slam and other stories (Dutch Edition)* by Leonid Andreev
- *METRO 2033 (Dutch Edition)* by Dmitry Glukhovsky
- *METRO 2034 (Dutch Edition)* by Dmitry Glukhovsky
- *A Russian Story* by Eugenia Kononenko
- *Herstories, An Anthology of New Ukrainian Women Prose Writers*
- *The Battle of the Sexes Russian Style* by Nadezhda Ptushkina
- *A Book Without Photographs* by Sergey Shargunov
- *Down Among The Fishes* by Natalka Babina
- *disUNITY* by Anatoly Kudryavitsky
- *Sankya* by Zakhar Prilepin
- *Wolf Messing* by Tatiana Lungin
- *Good Stalin* by Victor Erofeyev
- *Solar Plexus* by Rustam Ibragimbekov
- *Don't Call me a Victim!* by Dina Yafasova
- *Poetin (Dutch Edition)* by Chris Hutchins and Alexander Korobko
- *A History of Belarus* by Lubov Bazan

- *Children's Fashion of the Russian Empire* by Alexander Vasiliev
- *Empire of Corruption - The Russian National Pastime* by Vladimir Soloviev
- *Heroes of the 90s: People and Money. The Modern History of Russian Capitalism*
- *Fifty Highlights from the Russian Literature (Dutch Edition)* by Maarten Tengbergen
- *Bajesvolk (Dutch Edition)* by Mikhail Khodorkovsky
- *Tsarina Alexandra's Diary (Dutch Edition)*
- *Myths about Russia* by Vladimir Medinskiy
- *Boris Yeltsin: The Decade that Shook the World* by Boris Minaev
- *A Man Of Change: A study of the political life of Boris Yeltsin*
- *Sberbank: The Rebirth of Russia's Financial Giant* by Evgeny Karasyuk
- *To Get Ukraine* by Oleksandr Shyshko
- *Asystole* by Oleg Pavlov
- *Gnedich* by Maria Rybakova
- *Marina Tsvetaeva: The Essential Poetry*
- *Multiple Personalities* by Tatyana Shcherbina
- *The Investigator* by Margarita Khemlin
- *The Exile* by Zinaida Tulub
- *Leo Tolstoy: Flight from paradise* by Pavel Basinsky
- *Moscow in the 1930* by Natalia Gromova
- *Laurus (Dutch edition)* by Evgenij Vodolazkin
- *Prisoner* by Anna Nemzer
- *The Crime of Chernobyl: The Nuclear Goulag* by Wladimir Tchertkoff
- *Alpine Ballad* by Vasil Bykau
- *The Complete Correspondence of Hryhory Skovoroda*
- *The Tale of Aypi* by Ak Welsapar
- *Selected Poems* by Lydia Grigorieva
- *The Fantastic Worlds of Yuri Vynnychuk*
- *The Garden of Divine Songs and Collected Poetry of Hryhory Skovoroda*
- *Adventures in the Slavic Kitchen: A Book of Essays with Recipes*
- *Seven Signs of the Lion* by Michael M. Naydan
- *Forefathers' Eve* by Adam Mickiewicz
- *One-Two* by Igor Eliseev

- *Girls, be Good* by Bojan Babić
- *Time of the Octopus* by Anatoly Kucherena
- *The Grand Harmony* by Bohdan Ihor Antonych
- *The Selected Lyric Poetry Of Maksym Rylsky*
- *The Shining Light* by Galymkair Mutanov
- *The Frontier: 28 Contemporary Ukrainian Poets - An Anthology*
- *Acropolis: The Wawel Plays* by Stanisław Wyspiański
- *Contours of the City* by Attyla Mohylny
- *Conversations Before Silence: The Selected Poetry of Oles Ilchenko*
- *The Secret History of my Sojourn in Russia* by Jaroslav Hašek
- *Mirror Sand: An Anthology of Russian Short Poems in English Translation* (A Bilingual Edition)
- *Maybe We're Leaving* by Jan Balaban
- *Death of the Snake Catcher* by Ak Welsapar
- *A Brown Man in Russia: Perambulations Through A Siberian Winter* by Vijay Menon
- *Hard Times* by Ostap Vyshnia
- *The Flying Dutchman* by Anatoly Kudryavitsky
- *Nikolai Gumilev's Africa* by Nikolai Gumilev
- *Combustions* by Srđan Srdić
- *The Sonnets* by Adam Mickiewicz
- *Dramatic Works* by Zygmunt Krasiński
- *Four Plays* by Juliusz Słowacki
- *Little Zinnobers* by Elena Chizhova
- *We Are Building Capitalism! Moscow in Transition 1992-1997*
- *The Nuremberg Trials* by Alexander Zvyagintsev
- *The Hemingway Game* by Evgeni Grishkovets
- *A Flame Out at Sea* by Dmitry Novikov
- *Jesus' Cat* by Grig
- *Want a Baby and Other Plays* by Sergei Tretyakov
- *I Mikhail Bulgakov: The Life and Times* by Marietta Chudakova
- *Leonardo's Handwriting* by Dina Rubina
- *A Burglar of the Better Sort* by Tytus Czyżewski
- *The Mouseiad and other Mock Epics* by Ignacy Krasicki
- *Ravens before Noah* by Susanna Harutyunyan
- *Duel* by Borys Antonenko-Davydovych
- *An English Queen and Stalingrad* by Natalia Kulishenko
- *Point Zero* by Narek Malian
- *Absolute Zero* by Artem Chekh
- *Olanda* by Rafał Wojasiński

More coming soon...